Cross Your Heart
and Hope to Die

Words written by

Cynthia Jane Poulos

With Contributions by Michael Poulos

Cover design by: Dayna Kramer

Contributions by: Michael Poulos.

Acknowledgment

I would like to take a moment to thank those who have helped me with this book.

- ❖ My Husband, Michael. You're the love of my life and my best friend.
- ❖ My Mother, Lisa, there is nothing I have in my life that she hasn't helped with.
- ❖ Mike Poulos, Thanks Mr.P, for pitying the fool who broke her laptop. Love your daughter in-law
- ❖ My beta readers are amazing and I could never do what I do, without them. In alphabetical order because they are all equally amazing
  Alissa Reid, Alizé Cratch, Brittany-Anne Taylor, Courtney Kirtland, Debbie Wagner, Gina Fontenot, Jamie Boyer, Katelyn Knabenbauer, Katrina Rawlings, Natasha Hock, Shane Jade, and Rachel Pryor
- ❖ A big thank you to Sabrina Tompkins for editing my book. You're amazing.

⚠ TRIGGER WARNINGS ⚠
MAY CONTAIN SPOILERS.

The next page will contain a list of possible triggers and spoilers. If you would prefer not to spoil, skip the next page.

⚠ TRIGGER WARNINGS ⚠
MAY CONTAIN SPOILERS.

It is my sincere desire to provide you with fun and inspiring entertainment. However, this book contains themes that may not be appealing to all readers. Please consider an alternative novel if the following is content, you would dislike or find unsettling.

Blood

Death of a character

Drinking

Drugs

Dubcon

Explicit sexual situations

Flaying

Gore

Graphic violence

Gunplay

Hallucination

Knife play

Mention of suicide

Murder

Mutilation

Patricide

Strong language

Torture

Dedication

To all my Brats out there wanting a Dom to fight with while they put you in your place... Same.

Now turn the page so Mayan can tell you what a good girl you are.

Table Of Contents

Cross Your Heart and Hope to Die

Prologue

The brown leaves lying on the grassy ground of the park, signifying the end of fall, crunched beneath Gianna's shuffling feet as she walked beside Roman. She stole a quick glance at the handsome fifteen-year-old, then fixed her eyes back to the ground.

His dark locks peeking out from under the hood of his all-black, zip-up hoodie and his dark blue baggy jeans laying perfectly on top of his pristine white Nike's made him look like the older bad boy of her dreams.

She was only eleven though, not even a teenager yet. Even though she knew there was no way he would ever look at her the way she looked at him, she couldn't help it. She chastised herself, in her mind. *You should just be happy that he sees you at all. Happy that he's bringing you to hang out.*

Her voice came out smaller than she expected it to when she said, "So, this neighborhood doesn't look too bad." Her head lifted for a fast look around. "I mean, we are at a park."

Roman laughed. "Well, yeah, I mean, even in the bad parts of town, there are kids."

She inwardly admonished herself, *Stupid, stupid. Of course, there are parks*. She shook her head, and her eyes rolled. *Way to show how north side you are, Gianna.* Roman nudged her shoulder with his. Her dark eyes peeked at him through her black curls, and she saw a toothy smirk.

"Don't be so nervous. It's just my little brother and his friends."

She let out a loud huff of annoyance. "I'm not nervous, Roman."

"It's okay if you are," he said. "They can be a little rough. They aren't like you."

She scoffed. "What's that supposed to mean?"

"I just mean because you are, umm, I don't know, softer maybe?" He paused and then continued on hurriedly. No doubt he saw her body go rigid. "What I mean to say is, try not to let them walk on you, especially my brother."

She tried to pretend his words didn't hurt her feelings. She was the daughter of the Don. No one should ever doubt how tough she was. She shrugged and looked back at the ground. "I'm just sick of walking. I'm not nervous or scared."

He bumped into her shoulder again. "Well, it's a good thing we are here then," he said as he began to jog ahead.

Her eyes rose, but her head stayed down, as anxiety shot like electricity through her body as she took in the scene.

Just a few feet away, Roman stepped onto a paved area with two basketball hoops positioned at either end. Faint remnants of paint were all that remained of the lines, and no nets were attached to the hoops.

He slowed to a walk as he approached a younger boy with shaggy blond hair who sat cross-legged at the edge of the court, his face hidden behind a Game Boy. "Hey, Nickels, what are you playing?" Roman asked as he stopped beside the boy.

Gianna's heart gave a funny little squeeze. *He brought me here to meet someone even younger than me? Oh god. He thinks I'm a baby.* Her gut twisted with embarrassment, but she kept walking.

Loud grunts of exertion drew her wide eyes to the right side of the court, and her mouth went dry. Two dark-haired, bronzed, shirtless gods clashed in front of the hoop, their bodies gleaming with sweat. Her world turned rapidly, and the cold, damp ground kissed her awe-struck face while forcing the air from her lungs.

Gianna had been so engrossed in the moment that she had somehow tripped over the air and majestically faceplanted.

She turned her head and laid her heated cheek against the grass while she sucked in a hard breath. Laughter drifted on the wind, and a groan slid past her lips as she pushed her hand between the ground and her chest.

She heard an unfamiliar male voice coming from right above her. "Hey, you okay?" Horrific waves of embarrassment erupted from her stomach and threatened to bring vomit with it. She quickly rolled to her back, hoping she wouldn't need help. Her eyes opened, and the concerned face of one of the basketball gods stared down at her with his brown topaz eyes. He was squatting above her with his hands on his knees. *Oh, sweet Jesus.*

He raised an eyebrow. "Comfy?"

She tried her best to act like this wasn't the worst moment of her young life, and didn't want the ground to open up and swallow her whole. She crossed her arms over her chest. "Actually, yes." She attempted to put on a false air of confidence. "Laying on the ground is quite good for the spine. You should try it sometime," she said with a nod of her head.

He shrugged his bare shoulders and laid beside her on his back, tucking his hands behind his head and looked at her. "You're right. This is pretty good."

His voice lowered into a mock whisper. "Plus, if I do it too, hopefully, you won't feel so bad about that sweet faceplant." He laughed and looked to the sky. "It's probably the best I've ever seen."

Gianna's face heated, and her ears felt like flames were engulfing them. "Oh, so you saw that?"

"Oh yeah, but don't worry. I waved Roman away when I ran over."

"Ahh, I see. Was that you laughing then?" She asked angrily.

His eyes found hers again. "No, that was Mayan. I'm Dante, by the way." He sat up and offered her a hand. She reluctantly grabbed it and pulled herself to sit upright, then began wiping her face to make sure there wasn't any dirt or grass. "Sorry, Mayan can be an asshole sometimes."

Her eyes narrowed, and she shot him a nasty look. "I'd say so. Laughing at someone for falling screams, I'm a prick."

Dante got to his feet and offered her a hand again. "Yeah, but I don't think he laughed to be mean. I think he just watches too many stooge reruns." His head tilted, and he looked thoughtful. "Does that make sense?"

She didn't take his hand this time. She mumbled beneath her breath as she stood and wiped her pants. "Sounds like *he's* a stooge."

Dante laughed loudly. "So, then you do know Mayan."

Roman yelled from the basketball court to them. "All good?"

As the pair began to walk, Dante yelled back, "All good."

Gianna tucked her hands into the sleeves of her baby blue grass-stained sweater and then crossed her arms. *Just act like it wasn't that bad. One laughed at you, but at least they all didn't.* One hand came to her mouth, and she ran her thumb along her bottom lip as she thought, *If that Mayan kid says anything or laughs again, punch him right in the gut.* A small smile began to take shape. *Yeah, punch him in the fucking stomach and ask him how funny he thinks it is.*

Roman's voice pulled her from her thoughts as she walked to the center of the court. "Sorry, I didn't notice you fall right away." He put an arm around her shoulder and gave her a squeeze. "You good?"

Gianna's tongue knotted, and all she could get out while Roman held her was, "I, uh, well, I."

While jogging towards the hoop for a layup, Mayan laughed at her again. "Holy crap, how hard did she hit her head?" His feet hit the ground, and he dribbled the ball back to the center of the court.

He stopped before Gianna and Roman and dribbled the ball, alternating hands so it crossed from side to side. Then the most beautiful shit-eating grin she had ever seen spread across his face. "Or did the princess talk like that before she slammed her face into the grass?"

A fire sparked within Gianna and rolled through her. She took a step forward and stared right into his sparkling green eyes. Her hands balled into fists at her sides as she scrunched her nose up and sniffed. With a grimace, she said, "Yup. I figured that foul smell would be coming from you with all that shit you're talking."

His eyebrows shot up in surprise right before she stepped forward again and punched her fist right into his abdomen as hard as she could. The ball rolled away, and Mayan let out a deep 'oof' as he clutched his stomach and sank down to one knee.

Roman and Dante reacted at the same time. "Oooooo," rang out from behind her, and squealing laughter came from the side of the court. The little blond boy they called Nickels was holding his stomach and rolling on the ground, laughing.

In between bouts of uncontrollable laughter, he yelled, "You got beat up by a girl, Mayan!"

Roman pulled Gianna back by her shoulders and hugged her from behind. "Good job, kid. Don't let him fuck with you."

Mayan rose from his knee with murder in his eyes. He lunged forward toward Gianna, but Dante thrust his arms under Mayan's and wrapped them up behind his neck.

Dante's voice was strained as he struggled to hold the fuming boy back. "Heeeeyyyyy now. Let's calm down, okay?"

Mayan snarled and thrust forward. Gianna didn't so much as flinch. She stared him down with a smile on her face and pursed her lips to blow a kiss.

She taunted him in a sickly sweet tone, "Come get me."

Mayan's eyes flashed, and a cool smile spread across his face. He stopped fighting against Dante and just stared at her, his arms still awkwardly held over his head. For a second, Gianna almost thought she might have gone too far.

But then he spoke, "Nice right hook you got there." He jerked his chin towards her other hand. "How's the left?"

Roman's arms dropped from around her, and as Dante released Mayan, he reprimanded him. "You asshole. I swear you ain't got no manners."

She barely heard Roman whisper from behind her over her own blood rushing through her ears. "You did it. You're in."
Pride surged through her. She wasn't a stuck-up north-side princess, and now they knew that she had no problem proving it.

Chapter 1. Principe Demone

Loose ends

"Ya know, I always imagine peeling an apple during this part," he said, sliding the knife under the raw, blood-covered skin again. The man creating the earthly hell had a sick sense of humor. The gut-wrenching sounds of tearing meat were barely audible through the screams as he pulled at the meaty chunk of Howie's shoulder. Filleting yet another piece of flesh off the pathetic mess of a man.

Howie's tormentor stood straight and pushed the blood-spattered sleeves of his black dress shirt to his elbows. Further displaying the gruesome scenes tattooed on his large, muscled forearms. "Well, this shirt's shit now. Thanks, asshole." He said with a grunt of exertion as he stomped his black dress shoe into his prisoner's kneecap. A cartilage-crushing crackle filled him with delight as he watched Howie's eyes bulge with pain.

He began to circle his prey, flipping his black switchblade repeatedly and catching it deftly between his scarred fingers.

Like a lion lunging to take another bite out of a dying gazelle, the demon pounced, thrusting his fist into the already swollen shut eye. Rivulets of blood streamed down Howie Sicanaw's face.

Bound and tied to a metal folding chair, Howie's ravaged naked body was defenseless. The bite of the bloody, flesh-covered ropes eating away at the fragile skin of his wrists and ankles as he pulled at his restraints was secondary to the torture he was enduring. Guttural screams ripped from his throat, reverberating off the blood-spattered cement walls.

Ceasing his screams of anguish, Howie begged profusely to a God who would never answer. "Please, God, please. Please spare me. Oh God. I can't die. Please no. I'll do anything." An intense coughing fit took over, with chunks of clotted blood dripping down his chin and to his chest. His eyes fixated on the bloody protrusion of muscle that the coughing fit squeezed out of his split side.

Unintelligible garble poured from his mouth like diarrhea, falling on deaf ears as the demon examined his bruised, bloody hands. His lip curled into a snarl as he rubbed them up and down on the ruined shirt. Cleaning them before he pushed back his deep, black hair with both hands.

He let out a long, exaggerated exhale. "Ya know, I'm going to have to apologize. I know, I know." He said, raising his hands in mock defense. "I'm going pretty fast and hard, but I'm in a fuckin' mood. You got siblings?" he asked, quirking an eyebrow. Howie's only response was soft mewling into his chest as his head hung during his reprieve.

"Eh, whatever. Anyways, the only reason I'm doing this and not to some nameless soldier is because of my brother." He chuckled softly. "Well, and because of your brother." The demon began walking around the broken man, then playfully tousled Howie's hair. "You're a younger brother like me, right?" He asked rhetorically.

He didn't need to ask because everyone knew Howie was the baby of the rising Sicanaw drug family. Surely, they would be upset when they found out the baby of the family was tortured and murdered. But this was the kind of message one should expect when you openly defy the biggest player in Chicago since 1910.

He would get any information he could from the sniveling piss-covered worm, like warehouse locations and incoming shipments. But the most important piece of information he needed was the names of those who were still dealing with them.

After that, he would drop what was left of him at the eldest Sicanaw brother's front door. Of course, Tommy could retaliate instead of capitulating. But only if he wanted to lose another brother.

"They say we are the ones who are trouble, right? But man, it's always the older ones who need the most attention, isn't it?" Pointing to Howie with a questioning look, he asked, "Did you hear about the woman being gruesomely murdered in prison a couple of months ago?"

Lifting his head slightly, Howie softly cried, "N-n-n-no, no, no, I haven't. I swear. I mind my own, I swear."

A taunting laugh rang out in the small, dimly lit room. "Oh, come on. Yes, you have. I know you have." Shrugging his shoulders, he continued undaunted. "Well, you're going to die anyway, so I'll bitch to you.

That was my brother. He got all crazy over some dame that bitch fucked with, and little brother had to get him into the prison so he could satisfy his taste for revenge."

His lip curled in disgust at the thought. *Imagine being so into a chick that you ask favors and kill for her.*

After a moment, he was done trying to navigate his way through the foreign thought process, and he flicked his wrist, sending the knife flying through the air with precision. It embedded deep into Howie's quivering thigh, and he let out a voice-cracking howl.

Dark green eyes flashed with anger. Quick as a viper, he lunged toward the sobbing man and ripped the knife from his thigh, then ran the razor-sharp blade over each knuckle of the bone-white hand that desperately gripped the edge of the chair. Thick blood rained down from the excruciating wounds to the pool of blood beneath him.

"Okay, okay. I'll tell you everything. I'm sorry. I'm so, so, so sorry." Tears streamed down Howie's face while he snorted up ropes of bloody mucus. "Just please... Please stop."

Stalking in the shadows behind Howie, he waited just a moment before reaching his thickly muscled arm over Howie's shoulder. He grabbed Howie by his chattering chin and squeezed until his lips were pursed.

"Your pain is coming to an end, Sicanaw." Still holding Howie's face, he took the gleaming knife and dug into Howie's chest, creating a long diagonal slice over his heart. Deafening screams filled the room before Howie's head hung down again.

Enjoying the music of pain he was creating, he sliced into the unprotected chest again, finishing the flesh-carved X. A melodic whisper drifted softly into Howie's ear, "I promise."

Howie Sicanaw was one of the few unfortunate souls ever to be graced with the honor of receiving a Mayan promise of death.

The purple-tinted lights glinted off the swirling glass of whiskey. Mayan checked his watch while ignoring his partner in crime's unrelenting babbling. Dante and Mayan met when they were twelve, and they have been nothing but trouble ever since. As teenagers, they never undertook a task without the other, quickly acquiring a reputation for being Chicago's most dangerously unhinged pair.

Now that they were adults, not only did they share the same rank and title within the organization, but they also shared the same taste in daily activities. To them, it might only be three in the afternoon, but hell, the girls had to make a dollar, and they had to have a drink. Bass-filled music made ignoring Dante easy.

"Mayan! Hey man, are you even listening to me?" Mayan continued watching the topless dancer hanging upside down on the pole. *Maybe I'll take that one home tonight*, he thought. *I need a good release after last night.* She was a new girl with a pretty smile, big tits, and thighs that could smother him to death, just the way he liked his women. At least he would die with a smile on his face and a pretty cunt in his mouth.

Almost all the women at Geo's Gentleman's Club doubled as prostitutes. But he knew which ones were new and which ones were vetted. Mayan wasn't one to bring one of the vetted home. Dante did all the time and to each their own. But Mayan, Mayan didn't like playing with things that could be bought; the chase is what made it fun.

His shoulder jumped forward suddenly, sending whiskey splashing up the sides of the glass and onto his fingers, bringing him back from his thoughts.

"Fuckin' what, Dante?" Mayan snapped while shaking the liquid from his hand.

"You think it was her? You think she's in her daddy's ear again?" Dante's smile was big and mischievous.

"You know damn well she is, Dante. She's the fuckin' underboss. Don't get me going. Not now." He sneered as he sipped his whiskey and grumbled, "Dumb bitch." While exhaling the welcomed smooth burn.

The familiar feeling of a triple-vibration text heightened his agitation. Taking out his phone, he threw his head back and reiterated, "NOT NOW." Dante turned, peeking at the illuminated screen. His big ass mouth dropped open, and a mocking boisterous laugh echoed through the exotic dance club, even with the music.

"I'm sorry, Mayan, I know you're pissed, man. But this shit's always hilarious. Between your little cousin constantly needing you, and G, the permanent thorn in your dick hole, you can't catch a break." He shook his head and sat back with a whistle. "Shit's always hilarious."

His eyebrow raised as he leaned over to nudge Mayan's shoulder again. "How pissed were you when you found out she started targeting that candidate you were eyeing?" He covered his mouth in a fake attempt to hide his laugh.

●●●   82% ▰▰▱

  ‹ Messages   **Tanya**   Details

> Is there any way you
> could pick me up from
> school today? I don't
> need a lecture. But Peter
> took off with my car and
> is being a prick.

"Fuck you, Dante. You know she always has to try to one-up me." He rolled his eyes and mumbled to himself before looking down at his phone. "I swear if she weren't straight, she would be trying to fuck every bitch I look at too. Jealous ass cunt."

> No. And this guy sounds
> like a fuckin' mook. But I
> always got you. I'll send
> someone.

Without looking at him, Mayan responded to Dante. "You know, if you weren't my best friend, I would throw you across the fuckin' club. You stupid ass goon."

He looked at Dante. "Hey. Nickels busy? Or can he pick up Tanya?"

Dante's smile grew, and his hand raised to rub his chin. "You want Nickels... to go get Tanya... your..." He stopped, put his hand in the air, and turned his head down and to the side. "And I mean no disrespect." His hands lowered, and the smile reappeared as his eyes raised again. "Your thick-ass, blue-eyed baby cousin... home."

Mayan's head tilted side to side in contemplation. "You're right. It's a miracle he hasn't sniffed her out since she's been back anyway."

After sending the text, he slipped his phone back into his pocket and glared at Dante. "Seriously. She only came back because her mom died." He took a drink and then tapped his finger on the cup. "She's got shit taste in men. But she likes loser frat-type boys. Nickels' dumbass is the last thing she would go for."

"Hey! That's my brother, and-" Dante tried to defend his baby brother like he always ended up doing. But Mayan cut him off.

"Yeah, and you know he's nuts for butts and would be all over her. You're the one who reminded me." He said, throwing his arms up in exasperation. "He would hound her and probably do something crazy I would have to kill him for." He dropped his head to his hand.

"Ugh, he can't get near her. Dude has never even had a girlfriend. Only perpetual one-night stands with women even more fucked up than him." He looked up and pointed a finger at Dante. "I mean, I like that shit just as much as the next guy. But that shit's NOT cool when it comes to Tanya." Dante didn't continue the discussion. He simply turned back to the stage like a disappointed mother.

Dante was in no way a small man; he was heavily muscled and lean with a thin waist. Most say that he reminds them of a brick wall. But no one, not even Dante, would fuck with Mayan. He could turn off his emotions at the drop of a dime and he enjoyed torture. Plus, he was the Don's favorite. And the Don wasn't shy about it.

Dante's eyes didn't leave the stage as he stated, "So far, no word from the Sicanaws."

He crossed his arms over his broad chest and smirked. "But from what I hear, Tommy is beside himself."

Mayan's lips pursed, and his eyes lazily rolled. "Can't wait for the 'I'll get that bastard, Mayan' speech."

Dante shrugged. "I would hope he would know better than that. I don't want to have to paralyze him by busting his kneecaps with a baseball bat for threatening you." He pushed a hand through his hair and clasped his hands behind his head.

Mayan took a sip of the cool whiskey before adding, "If he's mad now, I'm sure he'll be furious after we intercept his shipment tonight."

Dante's large body bobbed slightly with a chuckle. "Insult to injury."

The steel door to the back rooms opened, chasing away the shadows of the club with bright light quickly catching Mayan's attention. The second he saw her walk through the door, a fire ignited, engulfing every bit of sense he had.

Mayan's eyes narrowed as he watched her make her way toward his table. He downed the rest of his drink, then signaled to the bartender to have another brought over. *I'm going to need it if the Ice Princess is coming to play.*

Gianna La Rosa, the underboss of the Chicago Outfit, walked straight to Mayan, her loose black curls swaying in sync with her plump hips. She didn't even pretend like she wasn't coming to bust his balls.

The purple lighting glinted off her deep brown eyes as they locked onto him, making his blood heat in anticipation of the oncoming altercation. It's said that Gianna's eyes are so dark that it's rumored that they deepen to pure black right before she steals your soul. *I don't think her eyes were ever brown to begin with. Evil bitch*, he thought with a smirk.

Gianna approached the table and sat, seeming completely unbothered by Mayan's glare and Dante's broad smile.

"You make up for that favor yet?" she questioned, grabbing the glass of whiskey meant for Mayan from the waitress in the hot pink fishnet body suit. The waitress looked at Mayan nervously.

"It's okay, baby, go ahead and walk that cute ass back to the bar for me," he said, sending a kiss her way with a wink.
She smiled brightly before turning on her heels and walking back to the bar. Complying with Mayan's demand, her strides more exaggerated than before. Mayan kept his eyes on her bouncing ass cheeks while answering Gianna.

Fuck her, he thought. *I'll show her my respect when she stops acting like a dumb bitch.*

"Not that it's your business, but yes." Turning his head to look at her, his eyes met hers, fire leaping between them.

"It's about time you do more than get your dick wet," she said with a sneer.

The buxom waitress walked up, breaking the tension and handing Mayan his drink. Staring unabashedly at Mayan, her lips pouted, and she pushed out her chest almost comically. A small dimple appeared on Mayan's cheek with his smile when he thought. *Oh, baby girl, it doesn't matter how big those get; you've had more garbage in your mouth than a raccoon.*

Gianna wasn't having any of it. Her dark eyes flashed dangerously at the waitress as she waved her away with a flick of her wrist. People might have been scared of Mayan, but Gianna, she was terrifying. When it came to work, and even most of the time in her social life, she seemed as though she could take or leave anyone.

Pleasant chit-chat, talk about your family, misspeak, and next thing you know, the woman you've known for half your life slit your abdomen open and watched as your intestines fell to the floor. Which, coincidentally, did actually happen.

Mayan took a deep pull of the whiskey. *I swear to God, she is going to give me a drinking problem.* "Last time I checked, G, I work for your daddy. Not you. You ain't the boss." He said, pointing a finger at her with the cup still in hand, then sipping again.

"You're right, Mayan. I'm not. I'm the fucking underboss. And you would do good to remember that when running your cock sucker." She said coolly.

"Mad, because the fella's down in boys' town were easier for me to control than you?" With that quip, Mayan purposely turned his head to the stage. A clear sign he was done with this conversation.

Dante scooted his chair back loudly and stood, blowing out an uneven breath. "Well, as much as I love listening to you two banter, we do have to go. Money to collect, a truck to catch." Dante pushed his chair in and nudged Mayan's shoulder. "Come on, big guy, before you say something stupid, and she shoots you."

Mayan gave Gianna a toothy smile and leaned forward, scribbling something onto a one-hundred-dollar bill. His voice was low and sultry as he stood. "Okay, G, but if you do, shoot me. I get to shoot something into you."

Her mouth immediately dropped open, and a huff of disbelief came pouring out. A look of disgust spread across her face as the pair walked away.

After gaining her composure, she called after them, "Mayan!" He turned his head just enough to see her as he continued walking. "I wouldn't touch you with a ten-foot pole and Dante's dick... And, I've told you before, don't call me that, idiota."

Not bothering to acknowledge her insult, he walked up to the new girl at the front of the stage and slipped the bill he had written on into her G-String. Slapping her on the ass, he turned back to G, flashed a sly wink, and licked his palm while he casually strolled to the door.

Exiting the building onto the busy city sidewalk, Dante shook his head.

"Seriously, Mayan, she's no lady. She will shoot you, and you know it. Why do you push her?"

Dante slid into the passenger seat of Mayan's black Lotus, and Mayan revved the engine. "I'd love to see that bitch try." Dante laughed loudly as Mayan pulled out into the heavy traffic and began to weave in and out while gaining speed.

Dante's head tilted in thought. "Ya know, I'm pretty sure Principessa di Ghiaccio needs a fat dick to shut her up."

Mayans face curled in disgust. "Her fuckin' pussy is probably as cold as a morgue." Pretending to spit, he continued, "You wanna freeze your dick off? Go right ahead, my friend. You couldn't pay me to touch her."

Dante shook his head, "Hey man, I've always thought she was good-looking." He pointed at Mayan. "You did, too, at one point, if I'm not mistaken."

The car took a sharp turn, and Dante flew forward as the vehicle stopped abruptly right outside their apartment. While fixing his white button-down shirt, he popped the visor down to check his hair, ensuring the deep brown waves were still slicked back to perfection and not dangling over the buzzed sides. "Damn, man, you drive like shit," he barked, still fixing himself.

Mayan got out of the car and bent down to glare at Dante. "And you talk too much. I never liked her. I thought she was good-looking when I was sixteen, and stupid." He slammed the door before Dante could say another word. If he did, Mayan might have punched him in his pretty boy face. He walked to the elevator angrily, making sure to press the button to close the door before Dante could get in.

Bringing two fingers to his forehead, he saluted Dante as the doors closed. *Fuck him.*

A minute later, the elevator rang, and the doors opened. Mayan walked lazily to his apartment, enjoying the silence. As he grasped the doorknob, he mentally prepared himself by closing his eyes and taking in a long, deep breath. It wouldn't be quiet for much longer.

Entering the sparse apartment, Mayan took off his black Italian leather wingtip shoes and attempted to sneak to his room. His black dress socks were no match for the cool gray slate tile that stole the heat from his feet as he carried his shoes to his bedroom. He desperately needed time away from the world. If Nickels and Poe got to him before he could get to his room, he might stab him… Again.

Sometimes, being on the forty-seventh floor wasn't great, like when the elevator goes out. But when he unbuttoned his shirt and plopped back onto his incredibly soft bed, the view reminded him why he didn't mind the trek up.

Rays of sunshine shone between the buildings of the skyline—*this city. My city is beautiful*, he thought as he closed his eyes. He took a deep breath and placed his hands under the brown satin pillow beneath his head.

Mayan exhaled loudly when he heard Dante slam the apartment door and scream, "Nickels! Why are you naked?!"

He didn't want to know what was happening outside his bedroom door. *Fuckin' goons,* he thought as he shut his eyes. Not even fifteen seconds later, his door swung open, and Dante approached his bed. Mayan kept his eyes closed and angrily asked, "What?"

"Are you going to talk to me about what's going on with your brother?"

Mayan's eyes opened and rolled with irritation. "Seriously, Dante? I didn't ask you to play couples therapist between my brother and me." He rolled over to his stomach. "Go away."

Dante pushed on Mayan's back, making him bounce between his hands and the bed repeatedly. "Come, on, Mayan!" He stopped bouncing him and put his hands on his hips. "I shouldn't have to tell you that you should be talking to Roman about how shitty he's been."

He didn't respond to Dante's childish antics. He pushed his face further into the pillow and clenched his lips shut. Dante sighed loudly and walked to the door. "This is stupid, Mayan. Have you even asked him why he's been distant?" Mayan pulled a pillow over his head. As Dante closed the door, he said, "Maybe he has something going on. Think about it."

Thoroughly aggravated by his friend's interest in his family drama, Mayan fell asleep thinking, *fuckin' Mama Dante.*

After two blissful hours of sleep, Mayan was startled awake.

"Mayan! Mayan!" Nickels yelled from the other side of the door.

Without opening his eyes, he reached further under his pillow, grabbed his twenty-two, and pointed it at the door. Cocking it, he said, "Nickels. Don't make me put another hole in the door."

"Oh, come on! I think I got it this time. Just let me try it out."

"Go try it on your brother. You know I don't give a shit if you perfect your Kramer entrance. Stay the fuck out of my room." Nickels huffed loudly.

"You're no fuckin' fun, Mayan. When you're gone, I'm going to rub my nut sack on your pillows."

Mayan's other hand flew out lightning fast, sending his knife through the previously punctured door.

Nickels let out a high-pitched squeal. "Mayan! That almost hit the jewels, you fucker. You hurt my junk; I'm going to make you kiss it!"

Relief filled him as he heard him stomp away and begin to knock loudly on Dante's door. *Good, bug your damn brother, not me. I have my own brother to deal with.* He thought as he reached for his phone and checked the text thread between him and his brother. *Still on read.* He shook his head clear and sat up in bed. Pushing his hair back with both hands, he sighed loudly. He didn't want to think about his complicated relationship with Roman.

"He never wants anything to do with me unless he needs something. And lord knows I'll do it." Roman and Mayan had once been thick as thieves. But it seemed as though when Roman chose to step back from the life, he also stepped back from him.

Determined to forget his family drama, Mayan got up and dressed to go to the gym. "If he calls me for a favor again and then ignores me, I'm telling Mom."

He angrily yanked his gray gym shorts from his oak dresser.

"Yeah, he doesn't want the life anymore, but don't be a rude bitch to blood. It's not like he has Nickels for a little brother." He growled in frustration, then put on his shorts and a black tank top.

Thoroughly pissed off, Mayan grabbed the knife from his door and flung it open, ready to hit the deck. As the door hit the wall, a giant black blur flew at his face. Squatting down so the blur narrowly missed him, he turned on his heels and stood. He stared at his dresser next to the gigantic window.

"Poe, you little shit. You could come in nicely, you know," he said to the crow cocking its head to the side as he spoke. "Great. He has me talking to him now." Mayan shook his head and chuckled. "You're lucky I like you better than your owner, Poe. I'll leave my door open while we're gone."

The bird only cawed loudly in response and preened a few feathers. He was pretty sure the bird was saying it was Mayan who was lucky that Poe liked him.

Grabbing his keys, he went to the living room, where Dante and Nickels sat on the black leather couch. Dante got up and grabbed his pre-workout shaker. "It's about time you wake up, Cinderella."

Nickels laughed loudly. "Bro, you dumb as hell.
It's Sleeping Beauty who gets put to sleep.
Not Cinderella, she's the one with the fat mouse."
He said triumphantly.

Dante put his palm to his face and shook
his head. "It's getting harder and harder to admit
you're my little brother. I think Mom and Dad
dropped you." His chin dipped, "God rest their
souls." He placed his hand on his shoulders, chest,
and forehead, forming a cross.

Nickels's face was the picture of
confusion. "What?!"

Mayan laughed loudly. "You're over here
schooling us on kiddie movies days after your
sick ass disemboweled a guy. That's what.
Something's seriously wrong with you."

Nickels smiled wide. "I know."

"You'll always be a few Nickels short of a
dollar, kid. But you know we love you," Dante
said, throwing his big arm around his little
brother.

Mayan huffed loudly and crossed his
arms. "Speak for yourself, Dante."

Nickels's smile fell, and his shoulders
slumped. "Ya know, Mayan, that shit hurts."

Mayan threw his head back. "Oh my god!
Come on. You already look like a bitch; you're
smaller than us and shorter. Don't act like a bitch
too." He looked at Nickels and pointed a finger.

"Only thing that keeps you useful is how fuckin' crazy you are."

Nickels bared his teeth and hissed, "You better watch your mouth, Mayan. Only reason I don't fuck your asshole with a dirty kitchen knife is because your Dante's bitch!"

Never one to stay out of a fight, Poe screeched loudly from the bedroom, grabbing everyone's attention for just a moment.

Poe's screech was like a bell in a boxing match and Mayan and Nickels lunged for each other. Dante barely made it in time to wedge himself between them and scream, "HEY! HEY! HEY!" His head whipped from one to the other, muscles flexing under the pressure of the men. "Let's not forget… You're both my favorite he bitch, in my he-man stable." Both men dropped their arms, and their straight faces mirrored one another.

"I hate you most, Dante," Mayan said, shaking his head and bringing his hand to his forehead.

As if her timing couldn't be worse, a triple vibration buzzed against his leg. Mayan's face hardened, and he hurried to take his phone out as they stared at him.

❮ Messages   Tanya   Details

> Thank you, My My. I miss you bunches and hope we can get together for lunch or something soon. Not knowing anyone really sucks. I wish I would have stayed with my dad as a kid.

> Sometimes it really gets to me, ya know.

Mayan quickly texted back,

> Maybe. Yeah, I get it. But you made out better than us. That counts for something.

He awkwardly shoved his phone into his pocket so no one would see the message. *My My. God, if anyone ever heard that, I would never hear the end of it.*

34

When his eyes finally rose again to meet theirs, they were staring at him like he had grown an extra head. "What?" He asked angrily, turning to get his shaker from the tight galley kitchen.

"Ohhhh, Ohh, I know who that was," Dante said, nodding his head with a barely hidden giggle.

Stomping back to the living room, he glared at Dante. "Shut the fuck up."

Nickels had both eyebrows raised to his hairline. "Anyone want to tell me what's going on?"

As Dante's mouth opened, Mayan cut in. "Just a cousin from out of town bugging me," he said, waving his hand dismissively.

Mayan put a hand on Nickels's shoulder and looked him in the eyes. "I love you, you weird little bastard."

Nickels's smile broadened, and his arm reached up to swing it around Mayan's broad shoulder. "I love you too, you big bitch behemoth."

Dante stood with his arms crossed, watching the two men he frequently claimed were his brothers. "Come on, ladies. Put your tampons away, and let's get to the gym before we run out of time before the job," he said before turning and heading to the door.

Chapter 2. Principessa

The girl

No one would guess that the withered man in the dark blue Ralph Lauren polo shirt who sat at the aged executive desk had more power than any other in Chicago. Giovanni La Rosa, the head of the Chicago Outfit, was once a domineering young man with the world at his fingertips. His thick black hair was now thin, receding, and white. His handsome face, with strong chiseled features now sagged with age and responsibility.

Giovanni lifted his tired eyes from the paperwork and locked onto the dark brown eyes staring at him intently. The princess of the family, his pride, and oddly enough, his disappointment all rolled into one, sat across from him. His daughter, Gianna. But she would never see him as the aged man that sat before her. In her eyes, he was still the handsome, young, solid Italian man who taught her how to tie her shoes and aim a gun.

Her father spoke, his voice a deep baritone, heavy with a Chicago accent. "Principessa, why were you at the club? I thought I told you, you don't have to be there to collect. You're above that. Send one of the men to ensure the girls are acting right."

Gianna looked down and picked a small piece of lint off the pants of her expensive black Gucci suit. Looking up at her father again, her expression was unreadable—a trait gained from being raised by a Don.

"They are more comfortable with me collecting. Being a woman, they are less intimidated by me." Giovanni raised a big, white, bushy eyebrow at her before his booming laughter filled the room.

"They don't know you're worse than the men then?"

Gianna smirked. "They know Papa. But if they have to deal with a cold-blooded killer, they would prefer it be a woman." She shrugged and adjusted herself in the chair, "I don't know, Papa, they're wacky. But whatever makes it easier, ya know?"

Giovanni's lips turned down, and his head tilted side to side. "Okay, okay, you do whatever makes it easier."

Gianna began to stand, believing the meeting with her father to be over. "Sit. I didn't dismiss you."

Her chin dipped to her chest. "I'm sorry, Papa, I thought…"

His face was stern, without a trace of affection. "That's the problem; you shouldn't be thinking. You listen and wait for me to tell you."

"Yes, Papa."

He cleared his throat loudly while cutting the end of a fresh cigar. "Did Mayan get the information we needed and take care of our little problem?" With the mention of Mayan, Gianna's back straightened, and her chin lifted.

"He did, Papa. I found him at the club today, eyeing another new girl."

"He's a good earner, that one. Let him take whoever he wants." He nodded and pointed his cigar at her. "Unless you want him?" He said questioningly.

Gianna's lip curled, and she nearly snarled. "Never."

"You should be nicer to him. He's ruthless, smart, and knows when to shut his mouth." He looked up as though he was imploring his invisible god, raising his hands dramatically. "If God had blessed me with a son instead of a daughter, I would hope he would be like Mayan." Dropping his hands back down to the desk, he proclaimed, "The best you could do for me is marry one like him."

He seemed to look off into the past. "I remember his first kill.

The boy was only fourteen, and he had just sliced through a grown man's neck." His head began to nod absently. "I was so proud of him. That's the first time I really saw Mayan and his potential. He was so calm, even as a kid." His smile grew, spreading from ear to ear. "That's the day I taught him how to do a Colombian necktie." Gianna's stomach curled tightly, and her muscles tensed at her father's admiration and love for the man who had ruined everything.

Giovanni took a puff off his cigar and rubbed his chin in thought as he let his mind play matchmaker. "Imagine if that was your husband." He smiled wickedly as he placed the cigar back in his mouth, chewing slightly. "

He doesn't have the blood to keep the Outfit in La Cosa Nostra, but you do. He has the respect and the strength though. He's only grown stronger since the day I took him under my wing and made him my Principe. Now pair him with you, and the Outfit stays in La Cosa Nostra, and you hold Il Principe Demone at your side." His head swayed from side to side with the thoughts of a powerful future.

Her face twisted with revulsion. No amount of strict upbringing could keep her face from rejecting every bit of that thought.

She tried her best to keep her voice from rising as she spoke through gritted teeth. "I am respected and feared by the men, Papa.

I don't need anyone to help me with that. Especially Mayan." Her skin tingled with anger. "With all due respect, Papa, Mayan's head is bigger than a Mac Truck."

Giovanni laughed loudly. "I remember a time you did need him." Gianna's blood ran cold with the mention of the life-altering memory.

Giovanni's head tilted, and his shoulders shrugged lazily. "Since then, you two have hated each other." He tapped his cigar over the ornate ashtray and stood, "Figure that shit out." He pointed a fat breakfast sausage finger at her. "He would be good to have with you. You're my daughter and the underboss, but that doesn't mean shit once I'm gone.

You have to take it. Having a man like Mayan standing with you will make that easier. And nothing makes a man more loyal than a good woman." He winked at his daughter, who was clearly uninterested in his ideas, and slowly walked to the coat stand. His limp was more noticeable than she had ever seen. But she would never mention it. All she could do was hope he would use his cane when it got bad enough.

Ralphy the bulky, bald bodyguard, and Geo's longest-living friend, finally moved breaking his statue-like existence. Ralphy and Geo didn't start off as friends.

Long before Geo was the Don, he and Ralphy met while fighting for the neighborhood beauty Teresa's heart. Everyone knew that while Ralphy would always hold a flame for Teresa, during that time, he gained respect for Geo.

Eventually, the mutual respect turned into brotherly love. Geo never moved up without Ralphy beside him, and Ralphy never let anything happen to Geo. These days, Ralphy acted as a sort of bodyguard for Geo. Gianna may have been oblivious to his deteriorating health, but Ralphy and Teresa weren't. Having Ralphy as his bodyguard gave him an excuse to help Geo when he needed it and to keep any young gun from thinking twice.

He grabbed the blazer from the metal stand and held it out for Giovanni to put his arms in, his rounded belly protruding from the coat. "You would prefer to marry someone like Ralphy?" he questioned raising his eyebrows at Ralphy's gleaming bald head.

Gianna laughed hard, harder than she should have. Slapping a hand over her mouth, she gave Ralphy an apologetic smile.

It was a ridiculous notion. But given that Ralphy had never married after he lost her mother's heart, Gianna didn't think marriage would be a joking matter for him.

"Papa. I don't need anyone to help take over when the time comes. Even if I did, I have Seppie."

Her father nodded his head with the cigar in his mouth. "We will talk about this later. Go see ya mother. She worries." Gianna stood and straightened her sleeves. "Yes, Papa, right after I pay a visit to the future mayor and maybe his wife if he doesn't act right." Her eyes shone like dark bottomless pools, and a toothy smile spread from ear to ear.

Gianna's black heels clicked on the cement as she stepped out of her red Mustang. She sighed heavily, looking at the home where she had grown up. The beautiful two-story Lakeview Avenue home was giant compared to her one-bedroom apartment.

Their house had five bedrooms and six bathrooms, all for two people. She walked up to the front door, thinking about her childhood here. She had never been alone. Even though she was the only child her mother and father could have, she never wanted for siblings. Her cousins were always at her house. Her favorite was her older cousin Seppie, who was also the only one that was actually her cousin.

She opened the large white door, and the scent of her mother's heavy perfume filled her nostrils. *Mom must have spotted me pulling up,* she thought with a smirk.

"Gianna! Bellezza. I haven't seen you in a week. Where have you been?" Teresa La Rosa was basically an older version of Gianna, except she had a fuller figure. Their similarities stopped at appearance, though. Gianna had always had her father's wild soul, sharp tongue, and explosive temper to boot. Teresa wrapped her plump arms around her daughter and squeezed her tight in a warm embrace.

Nearly smothered in her mother's black curly mane, she blew out quick puffs of air, attempting to keep it from going into her mouth. "Hello, Mama, I've been around. Just busy." She pushed her Mother forward to look her in the face. "Papa said you were worried. You don't ever have to worry about me," she said, squeezing her mother's shoulders before releasing her.

Teresa huffed loudly and waved the notion away. "Never. I know who my daughter is. It's your father that worries." She turned and spoke over her shoulder, "Come. Come. Let's go to the kitchen." Gianna ran a hand over the soft fabric as she walked past the red wingback chair and the off-gold oval table beside it. The many memories of curling up with her nose in a book on that same chair while waiting for her father to come home flooded her mind. She shook her head to dispel the memories. Trying to make it about anything other than her father, she told herself, *I think I read too much as a kid.*

She continued, walking leisurely behind her mother as she began to look around the house. It wasn't just a house, though. It was a home— just not Gianna's home, and it hadn't been for a long time. Teresa was so proud of it, and Gianna was so opposed to it all that whenever she visited, she often wondered if she was adopted.

The entryway and much of the house adhered to an ostentatious color scheme of dark red and gold. Her mother would make it worse whenever possible by opting for deep red with a gold filagree design, much like the heavy curtains that hung on either side of the door covering the thin windows. She couldn't remember a single time she had seen the gold tassels that pinched the center together move. Most things in her parent's home never moved.

She must have been walking too slowly because her mother called back to her, "Gianna! Come on. Move your ass."

She rolled her eyes. "Yeah, Mama. I'm coming." She didn't walk any faster. She intentionally slowed down with a smile and put her hands in her pants pockets. "Look at this place." Her eyes traveled from one wall to another and another.

There were photographs on every available inch of the walls. Some were black and white, wrinkled and torn with time. Others were more recent. Photographs of her mother and father traveling. She looked at a photo of her parents clinking champagne glasses in France. *She finally wore him down. He's traveled more in this last year than I've seen him do my entire life.*

As she continued down the long, wide hallway, she ran into her graduation photo and one of the last ballet recitals her mother ever made her suffer through. Her head shook slightly, and a sad smirk appeared. *God bless her. That woman tried... It's not her fault she got a defective daughter.*

She turned from the photo, set on getting to the kitchen before she was reminded of the many other ways she disappointed her parents. But she fucked that up too. She turned and walked right in front of the photograph of her and her father at her seventh birthday party.

She was dressed in a frilly pink dress that her mother had made her wear. She hated it so much that her father had told her she could wear anything she wanted underneath, and he would never tell. She ran a hand over the photo. In her eyes, his appearance hadn't changed a bit.

He would forever be the cigar-smoking superhero to her, even if he had turned out to be more of a supervillain. She pulled her hand back from the photograph as though it had burned her. He was staring up at her as he held her to keep her safe as she rode the pony. That was the last time he ever looked at her that way. The last time her father truly saw her and loved her.

She was jolted from her melancholy memories by her mother's voice cracking as she yelled for her from the kitchen. "Gianna! How the hell you get lost in your own damn home?"

She walked away from the paper painted with sadness and put a little pep in her step as she strode to the kitchen. *"Alright. You've made Mom mad enough,"* she said, but her father stayed on her mind.

Gianna walked into the extravagant kitchen, filled with every cooking widget, gadget, and top-of-the-line black stainless-steel appliances, with a question locked and loaded.

Without wasting any time, Gianna asked, "Why would Papa worry? I see him all the time." The short angry lady pulled open the refrigerator door and waved for Gianna to sit in one of the twelve chairs at the enormous black walnut dining room table.

"Sit. It's your father that worries, not me. He just doesn't know how to say it. You know he's not good with all that. But he loves you. Not to mention you're thirty-five with no husband or kids, and your boyfriend just ran off." Gianna's face tightened at the mention of the betrayal.

Teresa didn't take notice of her daughter's distress. Instead, she pulled out a jug of milk and brought it to the stone counter, then pulled out a cup from the cabinet above. "You want some cookies? Of course, you do." She said, not bothering to listen for a response. "I just made them."

A jovial male voice filled the room as Teresa walked to the table with the stacked plate of cookies. "Gianna! What are you doing here?" Giuseppe said, eyeing the cookies. "Oh, you could smell them, huh?"

"Shut up, Seppie. I think it's you who sniffed 'em out, tubby." She quipped, pointing to his chubby midsection while taking a cookie and the cup of milk.

Rubbing his chubby tummy and continuing down his thighs provocatively, he sang out, "The ladies love all the cushion."

Teresa smacked the back of Giuseppe's head. "Don't be nasty."

"Sorry, Zia." He said, rubbing his head and taking a seat next to Gianna. "Zia, I have a few things I need to talk to Gianna about. Can we sit and eat?"

Grimacing, she waved her hands at them. "Bah, I don't want anything to do with all that nonsense. I'm going outside to my garden boxes." Teresa didn't stay a moment longer. It was well known that while she enjoyed the perks of the life, she preferred to be blissfully ignorant.

Turning to Gianna, Giuseppe raised an eyebrow and bit into his cookie. His mouth was full as he said, "So, did you talk to the mayor?" Gianna's lip curled as she watched the crumbles falling from her cousin's mouth.

"Come on, don't be a slob." She said, handing him a napkin. "Yes. I saw him. I've been working on him. He was a little reluctant to cooperate." Gianna's eyes darkened, and her smile grew with the thought of her recent dealings with the mayor. "Well, he was... Until I realized I go to the same salon his wife frequents and sent him a nice selfie of us." Gianna shrugged and bit into the cookie.

"His wife? What did you do to his wife?" He questioned excitedly.

"Nothing, really. I sent them a message first. Hung bloody hands over the salon door. Then I told him if he wasn't going to be nice, I wouldn't either. It would be her hands next time," she stated flatly.

"Well, that was nice of you," he said suspiciously.

"Not really, Seppie. I took her pinky. Next time's the hands."

Giuseppe smiled while shaking his head. "That makes more sense. I didn't think you would be so kind. Zio will be proud to hear that."

Her face dropped at the mention of her father. "You know he won't be here forever, Gianna, especially with the life we live."

"I don't want to hear that crap from you. I get it enough from him."

"Okay, okay. Let's go out to dinner. We haven't been out in a while." He quieted his voice. "I know it's been hard for you since Stefan." Gianna stood and wiped the crumbs from her hands before grabbing her cup and walking to put it in the dishwasher.

Closing the door, she finally spoke. "I already have dinner plans, Seppie. And that piece of rodent shit, spit out by a chicken, never meant anything to me."

Light violin music filled the dimly lit room as Gianna swirled her glass of aged whiskey. She looked up at the classically dressed waiter when he approached her small table for two.

"Hello, my name is Troy; I'll be your waiter for the evening. Would you like to wait for the rest of your party, ma'am? Or order now?"

"You can take the other place setting. I am not waiting on anyone," she stated flatly.

He rushed to grab the place setting. "I'm sorry, I'll take that away."

Leaning over the table toward him, Gianna raised a hand to the side of her mouth and whispered conspiratorially, "Don't worry, Troy. I knew I was eating alone." Troy released a long breath, and his shoulders relaxed.

Sitting back in her chair, she smiled sweetly at him, "I'll order now. May I please have a small Caesar salad and the chicken coq au vin?" The smile dropped, and her hand raised, "But Troy... Please, don't bring it until I finish the salad."

Her hand dropped to the off-white tablecloth, and the socially required smile returned. "Seems kind of rude to bring out the next plate before someone is finished." Pausing for a moment, she handed the menu to him. "Doesn't it?" She said, with just a hint of malice.

"Of course, Miss LaRosa. I wouldn't dream of it." He said, pulling the menu tight to his chest. He began to turn away but turned back, fidgeting with the corner of the menu. "I'll put that in right away," he mumbled before he turned and hurried towards the kitchens.

A wicked smile curled her deep brown lips. *He knows exactly who I am. I'm not the silver spoon pansies you usually throw food at as fast as you can.*

Raising the lipstick-stained glass, she called after him. "Oh, Troy. Please be a dear and bring another."

Lowering her glass back to the table, she began to play with it and laughed softly. The swirling contents of the half-empty glass took away the distractions of the world, and her mind began to wonder. *People… People are pathetic and weak.*

She watched as she changed the rotation of the glass. The amber liquid became turbulent and splashed up the sides in a dramatic flourish before calming into a lazy swirl again. "I didn't need Stefan. And I certainly don't need Mayan… I never did." Her lip curled as her blood began to boil. "I bet he's down at that grungy ass gym instead of working. Probably chasing sweaty gym rat ass."

After a few glasses of her favorite whiskey and an excellent dinner, Gianna left Bonne Nourriture, determined to prove herself right. She knew precisely where the gym was. The Foundry was where all the younger made men went.

Those monkeys need to scratch themselves. She made a dumb, mocking face. *And lift the big stuff in front of each other to feel good. Pathetic*, she thought as she took a sharp turn down the narrow road the gym was on.

Gianna slowed and pulled into a familiar spot where she could see most of the gym through the large windows. Her eyes narrowed to slits, and her teeth ground when she spotted him. "Oh, look at that. Same as always.
Has to have Dante and Nickels with him all the time, holding his hand." She rolled her eyes. "Pussy."

Gianna watched him sit on the bench, stretching his muscles out. His tight black tank top made her uncomfortably aware of exactly how big Mayan was, but then again, it did every time she came to watch him.

As he laid back and positioned himself beneath the bar, his ridiculously noticeable bulge protruded, accented perfectly by his grey basketball shorts.

Dante stood above Mayan, ready to spot him, when Gianna saw an instawhore in tight white spandex shorts with a matching low-cut sports bra nudge Dante out of the way.

Mayans snake smile appeared as she leaned over the bar and pushed her tits up with it. Gianna's mind went red. *Look at him ogle some fake ass tits. And he's got that stupid ass smile he does.*

"Wait a second! Is that Sandy? Motherfucker, that is. Look at that dumb fuck smile at that idiota," she growled. Her hands tightened on the leather steering wheel and turning her knuckles white. "And that dumb bitch doesn't have enough sense in that head full of Botox to stay away from that loser." It was no secret that Sandy had wanted Mayan for years. But to be fair, there weren't many men in the Outfit Sandy didn't want.

Gianna pushed her door open and stomped to the white jeep parked on the other side of the road. Popping out a switchblade from her pocket, she squatted in front of the back tire and shoved the knife in. "Play stupid games, win stupid prizes. Maybe this will teach her to stay away from toxic shit men." Standing, she wiped her hand on her pants and walked to the next tire.

Having slit all four tires, Gianna returned to her car and took one final look at Mayan. Sandy was gone now, and his biceps bulged as he benched the impressive weight.

Excitement flared, and a low throb pulsed between her clenching thighs. She told herself the excitement was from slashing the tire and the mild stalking. But deep down, as she revved the engine, she knew it was him. She could lie to herself about what was making her hot, but she couldn't ignore her body's response to the man she loathed above all others.

Still fuming, Gianna sped the entire way home to get the hell away from Mayan and Sandy. After a less-than-quiet elevator ride with a man speaking far too loud on his cell phone, she was relieved to turn the knob to her apartment.

Deep darkness greeted her before her eyes adjusted a little, and she saw the moonlight spilling in through the balcony doors in her bedroom to the right of the entrance. Her hand slid along the wall, searching for the light switch.

Her finger flipped the switch, and the fan and light in the empty living room sprang to life, illuminating her space.

She closed the door and bent down to unstrap her heels and take her shoes off. Scooping them up, she stood and fanned out her toes, then scrunched them back up to crack them after being confined to the small space of the pointed heels all day.

After sufficiently stretching her toes, she tossed her keys onto the white kitchen counter as she walked to her bedroom. She took one step into her room and then stepped back out. She looked the apartment over. She didn't have any pictures, not a single one.

Hell, she hardly had any furniture except for a small circle table with two chairs and her bedroom set. As her eyes searched, she realized she wouldn't find anything even close to resembling the things at her mother's house here. She was just built differently than her. Gianna was like her father.

Shoving that depressing thought out of her mind, she entered her room. When the overhead light sparked to life, she looked around. It was pretty much the same in here. White walls, a simple stainless-steel bed, a nightstand, and an Edison bulb lamp on top. She specifically purchased only one side table.

She never wanted anyone to think they could share her bed for more than a night. Two nightstands felt like an invitation to imagine a life with her.

Gianna strolled through her open room to the one place in the entire apartment that didn't look like a model home for showing—her walk-in closet. In here, there was no need to turn on a light.

She had a motion sensor light installed so she wouldn't have to worry about it when her arms were filled with bags. The back wall was not really much of a wall anymore. From the ceiling to the floor, cubbies displayed her many shoes and heels. Silly little shoe stands just wouldn't do anymore.

She slid the heels into the only open cubby and turned to scan the walls to her left and right. Both sides were lined with clothes. It was all here, from formal dresses to crop tops and pajamas, and the closet was stuffed to the gill.

But right now, she only needed to find something to wear while she relaxed before bed.

After selecting her nightie, she grabbed her glass bowl from her nightstand and filled it with her favorite strain of cannabis, purple cake. She could never decide if it was the magnificent deep purple color that she loved most or the astounding body high it gave her.

After she pressed the last bit into the tightly packed bowl, she happily licked her sticky fingers and turned towards the bedroom door. Always one to think ahead, she ventured back to the kitchen to get a glass of whiskey. *Going to need something to combat that cotton mouth.*

Unlike most adults, Gianna didn't possess any glassware sets.
She had one long-stem wine glass, one whiskey glass, and one she kept pushed in the back corner of the cabinet. Her eyes passed over it for just a second, and she felt her heart skip a beat.

It was the McDonalds Flintstone promotional cup that Dante had given her. After they lost their parents, he and Nickels had to stay in foster homes. Dante was seventeen, and they wouldn't let him take his brother or the money his parents had left him until he was eighteen.

She reached her hand up and touched the handle as the memory bloomed in her mind. She was begging him to let her ask her father if they could stay with them. Or, at the very least, see if he could pull any strings, but the proud young man wouldn't hear any of it.

Dante held his head high and put an arm around Nickels. "I got this, G." He held the cup out. "I just umm… It's really stupid. But this is something I begged my parents for."
He looked down at Nickels for a second. "They brought us to see the movie, and then, as a surprise, they got us each one after."

Nickels and Gianna both wiped tears from their eyes, and Dante continued. "Anyways, I don't want it to get broken or lost while they move us around for a year," he said, then pushed it into her hands.
She looked down at it and shook her head as his name fell quietly from her trembling lips. "Dante…"

He let go of the cup and pressed Nickels into his chest, his tiny body shaking violently as he sobbed.

"Just keep it for us until I get a place. Please." But he never came to get it. Shortly after that, all their lives changed, and they never looked at each other the same.

Her hand trembled, and she quickly pulled back from the cup and grabbed her whiskey glass. Filling it, she yelled at herself in her mind. *You should have thrown that out a long time ago. Or at least give it back to him.* But she wouldn't. It was all she had left of the two boys she once knew.

After slamming the cabinet door closed she briskly walked to her room, ready to forget all her troubles.

The wind whipped her black locks as she opened the sliding glass door to her balcony and she took in a deep breath of the crisp night air.

Letting out a long exhale she went to her oversized white nest chair and sat, placing the cup of her favorite whiskey on the glass side table. Bringing her legs up she made herself comfortable sitting crisscross.
Her eyes closed lightly, and her face tilted up toward the night sky.

She began to take deep cleansing breaths through her nose, then exhaled slowly through her mouth. With each breath, she thought, *In through the nose, out through the mouth, in through the nose, out through the mouth..*

With her mind now as calm as she could get on her own, she reached over to grab the purple bowl and lighter, lifting her bottom as she did. The wind lightly nudged her red, slinky night dress up, exposing the exquisitely rounded curve of her ass cheek. Ignoring the goose bumps that rose along her upper thigh and cheek, she repositioned herself, brought the purple glass bowl to her lips, and pressed her thumb down to ignite the flame.

Inhaling deeply, as she watched the glow of the embers against the backdrop of the night sky, she reveled in the sweet burn that filled her lungs.

Letting her head fall back lazily, a large plume of smoke left her, drifting away with the wind.

She sat in silence, enjoying the sounds of her city while finishing the bowl. It didn't take long for the embers of the flower to refuse to share their entrancing glow again.

With disappointment on her face, she coughed softly and set the bowl and lighter down to pick up the cold glass of whiskey.

Watching as she swirled the liquid again, she wondered out loud. "I just don't get it. Why can't I love someone?" Tearing her eyes from the glass, she looked out at the city. "They're out there.

People who want the flowers, and candy, and holding hands, with pretty pink and red Valentine's Day love." Her head fell back, and she groaned, "Ugh. None of that seems appealing. Not even a little."

Every relationship she knew centered around flowery, rainbow puppy dog love. *Even Papa dotes on Mama, and he's colder than me.* Why couldn't she want someone to hold her hand? "All that, all that fucked up crazy, is why you can't have a relationship," she said with a shrug.

Weeelllll. That and being unbothered and unfeeling when coming home covered in blood, she thought with a grimace. The thought of relationships, needy people, and even her father, made her mind turn to Mayan. *Stupid fucker can't even go to the gym alone. It's sad, really.* Leaning back into the chair, she lifted her glass to take a sip. A tingling body buzz set in just in time to make the cold drop of condensation that fell from her cup to her inner thigh feel better than it probably should have.

Traveling down the crease of her leg and to her ass, it left more delightful goosebumps in its wake. Looking around, she bit her lip in thought, then quickly decided she didn't fucking care if anyone saw.

She brought the cold glass to the thin material between the whiskey and her breast. Needles of pleasure pricked every part of her body, immediately tightening her nipples as she dampened the material with the condensation. She rubbed the glass in a circular motion.

Her mind was still on Mayan. The way he lay on that bench staring up with that insufferable smile. Without consulting her consciousness, her mind and body began playing out the scene. As she took the glass from her chest, she pulled the dress over, exposing her sensitive nipple. Feeling the air caress the hardened peek, she set the glass beside her, balancing it on the cushion.

Dipping two manicured fingertips in. She began swirling the contents, so the liquid clung to her skin. Gianna leaned back and spread her legs wide, allowing her slick lips to greet the stars of the night.

In her mind, she pictured herself straddling the weight bench with Mayan beneath her. His cock already hard and pushing into her clit. In the real world, her fingers slid between her lips, running the length of her, like his dick would do while she ground against him. His arms would strain, trying to reach her. But he wouldn't be able to break the ropes holding him in place.

I would use him. Use every bit of that fat cock I hear about and then leave him fucking starving for me.

Dipping her fingers into the cup again, she closed her eyes and resumed her play. The combination of the body buzz and the hot tingle of the whiskey on her clit pushed her closer and closer to the edge. Her breath quickened when her slender fingers, wet with whiskey, plunged inside herself eagerly.

Closing her eyes, she imagined Mayan's mesmerizing green eyes locked onto her bouncing, perky breasts. Sliding the head of his handsome cock into herself, she imagined the delectable pop of the thick rim breaching her entrance. But she wouldn't allow him full access. No. She would tease him with her warmth.

"Please, G. Please. Let me go so I can fuck the bitchy brat out of you," he would beg. She wouldn't listen, though. Her smile would widen, and she would purr, "No, Mayan. I'm going to fuck the bitch out of... YOU!" Within the imaginary world, she slammed her ass down to his powerful thighs, driving his cock deep inside her making them both moan loudly with the pleasurable pain.

Gianna's fingers pumped faster. Curling them, she found her G spot and rubbed, making her skin tingle with the heat of her oncoming eruption. Her free hand pinched and tugged at her nipple, stimulating herself further and freeing her mind with her body.

Her eyes opened, and the rush of seeing the city as she fucked herself nearly had her coming. Her muscles clenched around her fingers, and her eyes closed again.

In her fantasy, her smile was feral as she circled her hips with him deep inside her.

"Fuck G, take these off so I can bend you over and show you what a real man can…" Gianna's fist slammed into Mayans face, cutting him off and making blood trickle down the side of his mouth.

"Don't tell me what to do while I use your cock like the dirty dildo it is." She retorted, digging her nails into his chest as she leaned forward so she could lift her fat ass and then drop it down over and over again.

He smiled a wide, bloody grin at her. "You'll pay for this, G." He said, thrusting his hips up into her while she slammed down, forcing him to bottom out painfully inside of her.

Gianna pushed her fingers in deep, pumping wildly. Feeling her muscles tighten and convulse, she thought of Mayan swelling inside her, filling her entirely and sending her into a frenzy.

She began imagining the pressure of his cum filling her. Her pussy spasmed around her fingers, and she fell into an inferno of flames, soaking her thighs and the cushion beneath her... Like she did every time she thought about putting that piece of shit in his place.

Chapter 3. Principe Demone

It's not just her

Mayan's Lotus came to a screeching halt on the street in front of the old red brick building. He stepped out of the car like he owned the place, not even bothering to close the door behind him. Dante was only a step or two behind after slamming his door closed on Nickels.

"Oh, real fucking cute!" Nickels yelled, crawling out of the black sports car and stumbling to catch up. "You're a real twat you know that?" Dante chuckled at his little brother while Mayan tossed his car keys to the young man sitting on a chair in front of the gym.

"Park it for me, will you Vinny?" he asked rhetorically.

Vinny fumbled the catch and stuttered, "Sure thing, Mr. Mayan, right away."

"Not once have you let me drive that fucking car," Nickels protested.

Both Dante and Mayan responded in tandem, "He's more responsible."

Nickels nodded his head and pursed his lips while shrugging his shoulders. "Fair enough."

A loud bing bong sung out as the three men entered the Gym. Mayan greeted the man behind the desk while reaching over and clasping hands to pull him in for a half-hug. "Johnnnnnny."

The burly, plain-faced blond smiled wide and hugged him back. "How you been, Mayan?"

Mayan broke the hug, "I'm good, John; let's settle up on business so I can get a quick workout in. I've got to catch a truck."

John put his fists on his hips. "Jesus, Mayan, are you guys trying to bleed me dry or something?"

Mayan's tone was cold as ice and dripped with venom: "No, John. But that could always be arranged."

John threw his hands up in resignation, placating the cold man. "Ho now, Mayan, I'm just playing ok. Follow me to the office, and we can sort this out."

Dante left Mayan to handle business and began walking towards the weights. Nickels stayed by the front desk and leaned over it to try to see into the back room. Craning his neck at the men walking away, Nickels yelled, "Get me a shirt while you're back there!"

With a look of utter disappointment, Dante walked back to Nickels. "Shut the fuck up."

He paused long enough to smack his little brother across the back of the head. "Now go hit the weights."

After warming up with some smaller hand weights, the pair decided to hit the bench. Dante laid down first, with a starting weight of two hundred pounds.

Nickels stood behind Dante's head as he huffed and struggled to put up the last rep of his set.

"Come on, big boy, get it up for me," his little brother said, mocking a seductive tone. Dante turned an even deeper shade of red and slammed the bar hard into its rest with a loud clunk.

A massive brute of a man from the next bench over set his weights loudly and approached Nickels, "Are you sure you're in the right place talking like that?"

In an instant, Nickels had the point of a stiletto at the big man's chest. "See that TV over there?" he gestured with his head. "How would you like it if the next time anyone saw you here, it was on that TV? You could be on the six o'clock news." He said, pushing the blade just enough to spill a couple of drops of blood, then mimicked a news anchor,

"Our top story tonight, local meat head found in multiple pieces throughout the city." He took a step forward, and the man fell over the bench behind him, toppling a stack of free weights.

"Christ, Nickels, what the fuck!" Came Mayan's booming voice.

Dante walked over to the man on the floor and commanded flatly, "Get up and leave. Now."

The brute didn't argue and scrambled to his feet.

"That mook was running his fucking cock sucker." Spat Nickels.

"I can't leave you two alone for one minute without everything going to shit." Mayan bit back.

Dante pointed to his brother. "Woah, don't lump me in with bat shit crazy over here,"

Nickels went to respond, but Mayan cut him off. "Not one more word; I'm not in the mood for your shit."

Chastised, he kicked at the floor dramatically and started stacking the weights. Mayan moved to the bench and got ready for his set.

"John give you trouble?" Dante asked as he positioned himself behind the bench to spot Mayan while he lifted.

"He was light," Mayan said, closing his eyes in aggravation as he pumped the bar.

"It's always something with these assholes," he replied and helped Mayan rest the bar.

Mayan opened his eyes when he caught the smell of cheap perfume and smiled when he saw a set of obviously fake tits in a white top resting on the barbell above him.

"Hey boys, making a scene again?" Asked the bimbo.

"Why? Are you trying to get more content for your fans?" Nickels said over his shoulder as he smacked his ass with a loose weight.

"We can't take you anywhere." Dante laughed.

Mayan lifted the barbell again and started pumping. "What's up, Sandy?"

"Oh, nothing; I just thought I'd come over here and spill the tea. Maybe take in the sights." She bit her lip and obviously stared at Mayan's gym shorts.

Furrowing his brow, Dante repeated, "Tea?"

"Jesus, Dante, are you like a million or something?" she teased. "Anyways, you'll get a kick out of this, Mayan. So, you know the Princess's boyfriend, Stefan, right?"

She tossed her blonde hair but didn't wait for an answer. "Well, I guess he got sick of the cold shoulder and left her on ice."

Mayan set the bar on its stand with a loud clunk. "Why exactly do I give a fuck about this, Sandy?"

"Because, Mayan," she said, drawing out his name. "Stefan didn't just leave; he skipped town, and nobody's heard from him since." She smirked and pushed her ponytail over her shoulder again. "Word is, he's hiding, waiting for the feds."

"That's not good," said Dante, running a hand through his hair.

Mayan thought Sandy's oversized lips looked ridiculous as she gave an exaggerated pout. "Can you really blame him, though? Who would want to deal with all that every day?" She crossed her arms over her chest and pretended to shiver.

Agitation flared in Mayan, but he smiled from ear to ear. "I don't know, Sandy. I'd say you sound jealous. But the last I heard, you were dealing with both of the Morelli brothers. And that seems like more than just a handful."

Nickels flipped an empty barbell on end and used it like a microphone while crooning, "Double pennnnnatratioooon," He flourished his hand and finished with a "Yeahhhhh."

All three of the boys erupted with laughter, and Sandy's face went red. She stormed off with a huff. "You know you're a real asshole, Mayan." Her childish rebuttal caused the three to laugh even harder. |

After the laughter cooled, Dante prodded Mayan. "Hey, you know, for a guy who hates G, you sure came to her defense pretty quick." |

Mayan fixed him with a stern look. "I told you to cut it with that shit, Dante. She's the underboss, and that asshole went against the family."

"I always knew that guy was a fucking twerp," Dante said, accepting Mayan's explanation.

"Yeah, and he had weird fucking hands," Nickels added. The other men paused and looked at him incredulously. "Oh come on, like you never noticed how he had little clammy girl hands?"

"You're a weird fucking dude," was Mayans only reply to Nickels. "Anyways, if that limp dicked, pencil-pushing whipping boy thought the Principessa was bad, he's in for a real treat when Geo finds him."

Dante and Nickels nodded their heads solemnly in agreement. Mayan opened his mouth to continue voicing his dislike for Stefan but was cut off by a buzzing in his pocket.

Pulling out his phone and reading the message, he thought, *well, my asshole brother still hasn't said shit, but at least I have a warm pussy to play with tonight.* Letting out a long sigh, Mayan got up and made for the locker room.

"Let's get out of here. We have work to do," he said over his shoulder.

After more than a few close calls in his line of work, Mayan learned to listen for voices and scan the peephole and the bottom of the door for shadows prior to entering. There's nothing quite like the greeting you get from a .22mm hello to make you rethink what you explicitly trust.

Shaking his head to compose himself, he knocked on the vintage oak door. *Fuck, having to get rid of the driver of that Sicanaw shipment got me all worked up and turned around.* His teeth ground together with agitation. *That. And the princess always getting into my shit. I need to blow off some steam.*

His thoughts were cut short when he heard a reply from inside the apartment.

A sultry voice called out, "Come in."

Mayan, always with more balls than brains, twisted the ornate bronze knob and stepped into the room, shutting the door behind him.

Pleasure pulsed through him when he turned to find the source of the seductive voice stepping up to him. MacKenzie, the curvaceous dark-haired beauty from the club, was dressed much more casually than earlier, but she didn't look any less appealing in her plain black tank top and yoga pants.

He quickly surveyed the room. Always good to know your surroundings. Another lesson he had learned the hard way. Meeting a not so friendly dog who had attached itself to his ankle because it didn't like that he was manhandling its owner was something he only wanted to do once. Plus, you never knew when a husband would make a surprise visit.

It was a quaint apartment with an attached kitchenette and adjoining bedroom. Soft light emitted from burning purple-red candles that filled the room with the scent of pomegranate. R&B music with a steady and hard baseline played quietly in the background.

Fucking cliche, he thought, rolling his eyes. *But at least there aren't pictures of a spouse. And, would you look at that, no sleeping dog to worry about.*

"Hi there," MacKenzie said, greeting him intimately with the soft caress of her delicate hands sliding up his lean sides and over his toned midsection.

"You're not one to waste time, are you?" He said softly, allowing her to touch what she wanted while his eyes followed.

She continued her exploration and shook her head. "No, no, I'm not."

Putting a finger under MacKenzie's chin, he gently raised her head to bring her eyes to his.

"Neither am I; I'm glad you wanted to play," he said smoothly. She smiled and started to respond, her words turning into a giggle as Mayan scooped her up effortlessly. Grabbing her butt, he hoisted her into his burly tattooed arms. MacKenzie formed herself to him and locked her ankles behind his broad back.

The mountain of a man took several steps forward and pressed her back against a wall, kissing her deeply. With her wrapped around him, he could feel the heat from her center dampening the thin fabric between them and swelled in response.

Breaking away from the intoxicating kiss, she spoke in a breathy tone full of want, "Me too."

Mayan looked MacKenzie up and down, thinking, *This girl is going to do great at the club. Thick, full hips, perky tits, tight stomach, big brown eyes, and hair just like G.* The thought of G, while he held her doppelganger against the wall, excited him enough that his body responded without thought. His hips thrust forward aggressively, and MacKenzie let out a slight moan while rocking against him.

"You like it rough, don't you?" he asked through gritted teeth. He stole her response with another firm thrust. Her hands pushed into his thick black hair, clutching tightly as he continued to bounce her against the unyielding wall.

Mayan pulled his hands free from under her plump ass and used the weight of his body to secure her in place. MacKenzie's excitement was lost on Mayan as he caressed every bit of her luscious body, roughly squeezing and massaging her ample curves, going wherever he pleased, thinking, *this bitch looks exactly like G... wrong eyes, though.*

He bit down on MacKenzie's lip, then pushed his rock-hard cock against her softness while envisioning G's black obsidian pools instead of MacKenzie's warm drops of honey.

MacKenzie pushed hard against his chest and sucked in her swollen lip, gently moaning. "Mmm, you're amazing, my clothes aren't even off, and my pussy's already wet enough to soak through my panties."

Mayan smiled slyly and leaned back, grasping the hem of her tank top with his free hand, quickly pulling it off and throwing it to the floor. "Close your eyes," he said sternly. MacKenzie did as she was told. "Now feel," he said, pushing her hands to his abdomen.

Acrylic-tipped fingers brushed over his bare, chiseled abs and traced the deep vertical indents where his torso met his hips. MacKenzie bit her lip as her fingers slid into the soft, dark hair that covered his pecs. Running her fingers through the curly hair, she greedily massaged his perfectly sculpted muscles.

As she worked the hardened flesh, her fingernails caught on the jagged scars that crisscrossed over his heart, and her eyes fluttered open. Mayan grimaced at her lack of obedience. "What are these?" she asked, running her finger along the marks. Mayan grabbed her wrists firmly, sliding her hands away from the scars.

"That's not a story for you." He responded coolly. Taking her wrists, he let out a low growl and settled her hands on the prodigious bulge contained in his trousers.

"That's ok. I'm more interested in this anyway," she purred while giving him a good squeeze.

"Down," he said while pressing firmly on her bare shoulders.

Without hesitation, she dropped to her knees, rubbing and squeezing his thighs and ass.

Mayan let out a deep moan of anticipation as he felt her lean in to kiss and nibble at his bulge while undoing his zipper.

"The girls said you don't disappoint. And I can see why," she purred.

Mayan imagined G kneeling in front of him as he unclasped his belt and popped loose the button of his pants. "Be a good girl and take it out."

MacKenzie looked all too happy to do so and pulled down hard on his waistband, eager to unsheathe him. Springing forward, Mayan's girthy, erect cock bobbed, then stood straight out in the air, throbbing for his dark-eyed princess.

He watched as her eyes went wide as she noticed the sparkle of jewelry. Mayan wore eight steel studs, tipped at either end with a small ball bearing. They ran along the underside of his dick and were each spaced about half an inch apart. *Deer in the headlights look is always a winner,* he thought with a chuckle.

Smiling triumphantly, he put his closed fists on his hips. "Ribbed for your pleasure."

Laughing, MacKenzie grasped around the base of his cock, tipped it upward and started to lick. Mayan's head tilted back in response, and his eyes rolled before squeezing shut. She moved her broad, slick tongue slowly. Beginning at the bottommost stud, she worked up the ladder's rungs like she was desperately lapping up a melting ice cream cone.

He envisioned G's soft, shit-talking mouth around him and placed his hands one over the other on the back of her head. He pulled her closer and pumped himself forcibly into her.

In the present, Mayan's hands and hips mocked his fantasy. MacKenzie was unaware that he wasn't truly with her and eagerly accepted his movements.

Roughly thrusting into her as far as he could, Mayan snarled, "I'm going to teach you some fuckin' manners."

MacKenzie moaned and gagged around him as he pushed his fat head past her uvula and deep into her throat. The sweet sensation of the warm muscles of her throat contracting around him made him want to push deeper into her.

Unable to accommodate his entirety, she placed her hands against his thighs and pushed back.

He didn't notice her resistance, gags, or coughs and didn't slow as he administered his lessons by roughly using her mouth and throat.

Of course he couldn't just enjoy this. She would never let him. He heard G, *look at you, not man enough to find a real woman? Have to keep playing with all these girls from the club?*

Lost in his delusion and determined to teach G some respect, Mayan picked up his pace and bit out between each thrust. "The way you run that mouth makes me want to feed you every last inch of my fat cock."

He clutched the back of her hair tightly and wrapped his large hand around her throat. He felt his fat dick stretch her and shook her roughly back and forth to work her tight throat over every bit of him.

Unable to endure the vicious skull fucking session any longer, MacKenzie pushed off his tree trunk-sized thighs as hard as she could.

After dislodging his dick from her throat, she nearly vomited, and after a moment of ragged breathing, she wiped her lips. "I don't think I've ever had such a mouthful."

Torn from his fantasy, Mayan looked down at the disturbance. Anger filled him when he saw watering golden eyes looking up at him.

MacKenzie was a mess. Her eyeliner and mascara had run over her cheeks and down to her chin.

His only consideration was that *G would probably show more respect if I made her look like that.*

"We need to take this to the bedroom," Mayan said while stepping back and out of his pants. He left them on the floor but paused momentarily to bend down and grab something from his pocket.

MacKenzie stood up and tried to collect herself but let out a loud, excited squeal when Mayan grabbed her by the waist and effortlessly slung her over his shoulder. He hooked the pink leopard-print waistband of her leggings and black thong with his fingers and pulled down firmly, snapping the thong and removing the leggings as he marched them both to the bedroom.

Once inside, he tossed her onto the plush bedspread. Standing well over her at the foot of the bed, he let out a low guttural moan while working one rough hand along the substantial length of his cock. Mayan wasn't looking at that, though. Instead, his eyes were on his other hand. Where he was tapping out a quick text on a cell phone and tossed it carelessly to the side when he was done.

"What was that?" asked an annoyed and nearly naked MacKenzie.

"Work," Mayan replied curtly, and he fixed the woman with a hardened stare.

"You don't seem too bothered, though," Mayan said, softening his expression when he saw her stare glued to his cock.

Agitation arose in Mayan when he noted her honey-colored pools again, and he shifted his gaze to her fully exposed mound. "I'm going to use every bit of you, especially this part. And I'm going to give you a lot more than just an eyeful, Princess."

He envisioned G superimposed onto the woman in front of him and poised himself on his knees between her spread legs. He could feel and smell the delicious heat of excitement rising from her core. And his cock throbbed and dripped with want. "I can feel how much you want me, Princess."

He closed the rest of the space between them and pressed his rippled, broad chest to hers, whispering in her ear, "I'm going to make you into such a good girl."

His firm, muscular thighs overpowered MacKenzie's half-hearted attempt at modesty.

She moaned as he moved his head to the top of her slit and started sliding up and down her most sensitive spot. "But first, you're going to beg me for it. You're going to demand I teach you."

She let go of herself and clawed at Mayan's back, leaving long red marks wherever her fingers could.

He winced at the exquisite blend of pleasure and pain when he felt her sink her pink-painted coffin nails into his firm ass cheeks. He closed his eyes and savored the hot burning sensation from her raking hands drawing blood.

MacKenzie pulled at his cock with both hands and tried to push the head inside of herself. He took her wrists firmly, lifted them above her head, and pinned them down to the bed.

"If you want to play, then we play my way." He said in a commanding tone that left no room for debate. "Turn over and get on all fours."

His perverse desire to continue his fantasy was satiated when MacKenzie complied with his demands. He smacked her ass hard enough to leave a welt, cherishing the sound.

"You need this, don't you?" he said, gently pushing forward with his cock positioned against her opening.

"Mhmm!" was all she could manage to say.

"Say please!" he demanded.

"Please, Mayan, please take me, make me your good girl!" she pleaded.

A deep, growling moan of satisfaction poured from Mayan as he drove forward, burying himself to the hilt inside her.

G, echoed the moan in his mind, saying, "I'll give you everything." He rocked his hips in and out slowly, taking every bit of her for himself. MacKenzie's arms collapsed under the force of his bulky body, her face buried in the soft bedding.

"You love the way I fill you. Don't you?" MacKenzie moaned something completely unintelligible through the blankets. And Mayan laughed loudly. He smacked her ass savagely again and thrust into her over and over again with abandon as her muscles seized from the pain of his palm.

"You belong here, on your knees, taking this thick dick like the dirty little slut you are, don't you?"

"I do!" cried Gianna in MacKenzie's voice.

Mayan went on, "You need me to own every last bit of you, don't you? You want me to use you until I break you."

He felt her body quiver as waves of liquid heat rolled through her like undulating ocean crests crashing all along the length of his cock.

He grabbed her waist tightly with one hand and pulled back hard on her hair with the other. Using the makeshift reins, he pummeled her ass with hard stinging slaps the symphony of wet slaps, moans, and pelting reverberated throughout the apartment. And with the song's crescendo, he felt the rise and fall of her lust again. He leaned in and bit down on the soft skin of her shoulder, heightening the wave of pleasure he could feel her riding.

"Oh, god, oh god, yes, fuck me, Mayan!" she cried.

Mayan growled like a man possessed by a hell cat as he pounded into her spasming body. Every word, every moan, every breath he heard was G's now. And each and every thrust he delivered was another lesson he needed to teach her.

MacKenzie's moans were loud enough to wake the dead when she turned her head to look back at Mayan. He was so enraged by her golden eyes that he pushed her face back and pressed firmly at the base of her neck, driving her head down hard into the bedding. He straightened his back and got to his feet while still inside her.

"I didn't tell you to fucking move," he growled, using his new upright position to deliver punishing thrusts for her insolence. Mayan worked her so hard that when his firm abdomen smacked her backside, her head would have bounced up and down like a ragdoll being devoured by a pitbull if he wasn't using it for balance.

"You're going to learn to fuckin' obey!" He yelled.

He felt the light slaps on his hands several times from the struggling woman beneath him. She needed to breathe and was desperately trying to get him to allow her a small reprieve. He reluctantly released his press but did not relent in his thrusting. His pounding hips forced her up the bed inch by inch until he had her against the headboard.

He bounced her off of it with a loud thump and commanded, "Work my cock with that pretty little fuck box, bitch." MacKenzie's body obeyed without question. Exactly the way he wished Gianna would behave.

Mayan leaned back and looked up at the ceiling as her spasms and final climax worked his rock-hard swollen cock. He felt the muscles under his aching balls begin to tighten in preparation and withdrew himself.

He closed his eyes as he pumped his throbbing dick with both hands wrapped tightly around it.

"You don't deserve this. But I'm going to give it to you anyway."

The wet slickness of her cum covering him let his hands glide effortlessly up and down his pulsing cock.

Then with one last stroke, he tightened his grip and released, painting her back with hot sticky ropes of cum.

Before he could even catch his breath, Mayan's phone began to vibrate. It was Dante. The text always worked, Mayan thought.

The two men had devised this ingenious plan when they were still stupid boys. During a hook-up, you could send a text that only said call and then a set amount of time. At that point, they could answer and have a good excuse to simply get up and leave. You couldn't exactly turn down work when the Outfit was calling the shots.

Mayan hit the decline button; *I don't need your help this time, bud.*

After getting dressed, he made his way to the door, looked back at the bed, and saw a thoroughly fucked MacKenzie already fast asleep. *Fucking ice princess,* was all he thought. And he closed the door on his throwaway toy.

The brisk night air whipped through the open windows, nipping at Mayan's face while he casually cruised through the city. Usually, he would have put on some music and ripped through town like a demon, flashing his shark's smile to taunt whores and cops alike. But tonight was different and he instead found himself leisurely taking in the skyline and sights while reminiscing.

When he hit Lower Wacker Drive, it was uncommonly open, and his mind projected a series of home movies against the tunnel walls.

He narrated the moving images as he slipped through the times long gone. *We used to hotwire a car and drive around like this—her, me, Roman, Dante, tiny-ass Nickels.*

Seeing the bobble-headed-big-toothed-little-psychopath playing with a switchblade in the backseat, he let out a chuckle and shook his head.

He remembered the time Francesco Capeli had told Nickels that his big ass front teeth made him look like a fucking rat.

And then he remembered how he and Dante held that kid down while the others watched Nickels stick an actual live rat in Francesco's cunt mouth. His rugged jawline flexed, *we always had each other's backs, and nobody got away with fucking with us.*

As the movies kept playing, he saw the five of them on the concrete screen, running around the city like it was their own private playground. With a smile, he thought, *we were thick as thieves.* He felt it was fitting since they would lift nearly anything that wasn't nailed down just for the hell of it.

Clip after clip ran along the walls following his drive. He saw them all grow older, and he watched as all the lessons that life had given them shaped them into who they were now. Those dark memories made his eyes glisten and reflected the trailing tunnel lights.

He wondered, *First G, then Roman. How long until Dante and Nickels take off, too?* Mayan hardened his expression, scoffed, and wiped his welling eyes on his sleeve. *Ah, who fucking needs them anyways?*

It wasn't long before the road took him and his contemplations where they always did.

It was the place he knew he wanted to go most, but he could never admit that, even to himself. Usually, he would fantasize about going up and giving her a piece of his mind, and sometimes, he would think about giving her a lot more than that.

His knuckles whitened around the steering wheel as he slowly passed G's apartment. He looked up at the fiftieth-floor balcony, and something else came to mind.

She didn't deserve to be run out on like that, even if she is a cold bitch. That pussy Stefan is on borrowed time.

Mayan scratched at the scars on his chest uneasily as his mind filled with white-hot rage. He sped off into the night, recalling what his big brother had said to him while wrapping a roll of gauze tightly around his wounded chest. "Christ, Mayan, he really did a number on you, didn't he?" When he didn't answer, Roman kept tending his wounds. "It's going to be okay, little bro. Just keep a shirt on, and our moms won't even know. Alright?"

A loud, old-fashioned car horn sounded throughout the car, ringing in his ears and tearing him from his memories. He pulled up the curb in front of the building he frequently found himself at and parked.

Would she walk out for a late-night drive? Would he visit her apartment door to press himself against it for just a moment in the hopes that he might hear her laugh? He never knew what he would end up doing, but he always knew he would end up here most nights.

He shook the thought free from his mind and quickly pressed 'accept call' on the dashboard touch screen, knowing exactly who that odd little tone belonged to. "Uncle Tony! What's going on?"

A low grunt of agitation and exertion sang out through the car speakers, and the image of his uncle putting a hand to his round, beach ball belly as he adjusted in the chair at his desk was crystal clear.

"Don't play small talk with me, kid. You asked me to take care of the patrol cars tonight while you handle that Sicanaw deal, right?" Uncle Tony had been a cop for over thirty years. Mayan's mom was fond of saying that her brother was a no-nonsense prick before he ever knew he even wanted a badge. Uncle Tony might be a no-nonsense prick of a cop, but he had added the adjective dirty to that title after only his second year on the force. That made Tony remarkably useful to the Outfit.

Mayan chuckled, and his eyes drifted up the building. He briefly wondered if she was on her balcony or sprawled out in her bed. As he wondered, he continued his conversation. "Yeah, I did, you cranky, old bastard."

"Well, you won't have any problems from the blue tonight."

Mayan's finger ran along the steering wheel while he weighed out the pros and cons of opening the unlabeled, expired can of worms that was his family drama. *Fuck it.* "Hey, you talk to Roman?" He paused for a moment and bit his lip.

He had to push down his anger before he continued. "He, uh, hasn't talked to me since he asked for that help."

Tony's response was immediate and absolute. "Fuck that guy. He don't talk to nobody unless he needs something." He let out a small huff that could almost be described as a laugh, but not quite. "Only time I see him is when he comes around the station, snooping around for information." It sounded like he spit before he continued. "If I was you, I would block his number. You don't need him, Mayan."

Mayan grimaced. *Well, that was a mistake.* "Yeah, you're probably right. Thanks for the help. I'll give Tanya something nice to bring home to you."

Tony grunted again and smacked his lips together. "Alright, kid. Don't mess this shit up. It could get real messy with the Sicanaw boys if you don't play it just right." In his mind's eye, Mayan could see Tony as he spoke. He would be leaning back, scrunching up his face, squinting his eyes, and pretending to throw a dart right at the center of his imaginary bulls-eye.

He grinned at the image. "Don't worry. I got those shmucks right where I want them." He turned off the car and decided he would take a quick walk around her building. *I just need some fresh air.* "Alright, I have some business I have to get to. I'll talk to you later, Uncle Tony. Let Tanya know she has to get ahold of me to pick up your gift."

There was a long stretch of silence before he heard a fast grumble almost too low to hear. "I'm proud of you. You started out on the bottom and made it big. Now you're a man holding your spot on top with an iron fist." His voice suddenly grew obnoxiously loud and angry. "Don't go and fuck it up by dying, shit stain."

And then the call ended, leaving Mayan with a perplexed look on his face, while his eyes blinked wildly, as if it was going to somehow make what just happened make more sense. He closed his eyes and massaged the lids lightly with his fingertips as he rubbed his palms on his face.

Cynthia Poulos

His words were muffled and sounded awkward, "What the fuck was that?" He pushed the air from his lungs dramatically and looked back up to where he knew Gianna's apartment was, and decided it was a bad idea to be there. *Don't... Your family tree has enough nuts. No need to go out there and hope to catch a glimpse of her so you can hate fuck your hand about it later.*

He started the car again and pulled away from the curb, thinking about what had just happened between him and his uncle. As kids, Roman and Mayan didn't have a father. Their parents were their Mom and Mother. They never complained and still wouldn't. Their moms loved them fiercely and tried their best to raise resilient, resourceful men. Mayan thought they had succeeded in those two areas, maybe a little too well. But try as they may, Mayan and Roman had some things for which they craved a male role model for. Roman needed that guiding hand more than Mayan, probably because while he had Roman to look to, Roman had no one without Uncle Tony.

Their Mother always said, "It takes a village, guys." Or at least she did until she realized that her bright young boys were making some very dangerous life choices.

It took her longer than it should have to realize that those choices were based on her brother's guidance. Had she seen it sooner, she might have been able to steer them in a different direction.

But she couldn't have known the nefarious activities her brother was partaking in while he took the boys on ride-a-longs. He and his high-maintenance wife kept their life of crime hidden from the world.

As adolescent boys, they saw their uncle living the life of a dirty cop in Chicago on more than a few occasions. Their wide eyes would almost sparkle whenever he would park his cruiser at the entrance of a dark alley, disappear into the night for a few moments, and then come back counting hundreds of dollars gleefully. They would get a sly wink from the muscular man with barely noticeable thinning hair after he shut the door, and then he would turn up the music, close his eyes, and lean back while placing his hands behind his head.

"Sometimes it pays more to look away than it does to play the hero."

Both boys knew from a very young age that they didn't want to play the nice guy like their father had. According to their parents, he was an upstanding man who helped them to make their family, and then tragically died in a mugging.

To them, it was never a question. The hero was the villain's fool. While the hero played by everyone's rules and wasted his life boxed in at a cubical, the villain was a man who made his own rules and spit on the laws of lesser men. Once they had grown into angsty young men looking to make their mark on the world, Uncle Tony was there to open the doors to the world of crime.

Chapter 4. Principessa

Her past

The rich smell of tobacco, spices, and leather filled the room as Giovanni exhaled, staring angrily at his daughter while tapping his fingers impatiently.

Gianna sat uncomfortably across from him in one of the two wooden chairs with dark green cushions. She was stuck between being annoyed that she didn't know why she was there and being obedient by not asking and waiting to be spoken to.

Finally sick of wasting her time, Gianna went to speak. "Papa…" The door swung open behind her before she could finish her sentence, and her father's face brightened.

"Mayan! Come, come, sit down." He waved a hand towards the open chair excitedly.

Mayan lazily walked past the statue-like man, Ralphy, and gave him a respectful nod, receiving one in turn. Sitting down casually in the chair next to Gianna, he greeted the Don.

"Geo. How have you been?"

"Ahh, damn legs have been acting up. Getting older and fatter. Ya know, the good stuff."

Mayan chuckled. "To what do I owe this pleasure, Geo?"

Gianna sneered as she watched the casual interaction. *I sit here for ten minutes with nothing more than a head nod and a pissed-off look, and this dick bag shows up late and gets a fuckin' smile?!* Gianna was pulled from her envious thoughts with the sound of her father loudly clearing his throat.

"It's not pleasure. Not even a little." He said, shaking his head. "I'm sure you have heard about Stefan leaving?"

Gianna's face flushed with embarrassment. *Why?! Why would he talk about that with Mayan?*

"I have. It's a shame," Mayan said with a 'tisk'.

Gianna couldn't bite her tongue any longer. "Papa, if you don't mind, I would like to know why you had me come here to watch you tell Mayan what happened."

Giovanni's face reddened, and his lips thinned as he spoke through gritted teeth. "It's your boyfriend running out that made it so you two had to be here." Gianna's shoulders dropped just a fraction as she took the insult silently.

Mayan cut in, "So he ran off. Send someone after him. I gotta be honest here, Geo. I'm not sure why we are here either."

If Gianna hadn't been one hundred percent positive that she and Mayan hated each other, she would have sworn he was trying to deflect her father's anger.

Giovanni smoothed what was left of his hair back with his hand, then directed his attention to Mayan. "Listen, Gianna fucked up." Gianna's mouth opened, but her father pointed the pungent cigar at her.

"Shut your mouth if you know what's good for you." Dark pools bored through Giovanni as she bit her lip, trying to keep her temper at bay.

"Piece of shit skipped out. Thinks he can leave the life. I know what happens when you try to do that," Mayan said. Shrugging his shoulders and shaking his head, he continued, "But I still don't understand what that has to do with me."

"As I said, she fucked up. She shouldn't have been involved with that jadrool." Giovanni looked down at the desk and spoke softly, "People say it's because he saw too much being with Gianna. He couldn't handle it all." His eyes darkened, and there was an edge to his voice. "I've gotten word that he's waiting in Vegas for the fuckin' feds to scoop him."

The room was eerily silent; not even his large exhale of smoke dared to make a sound.

Finally, raising his tired brown eyes, he stared her down, daring her to defy him. "That's why you have to go and fix your problem. No one has ever turned on the Outfit."

Gianna stared him down as she gripped the arms of the chair hard enough to whiten her knuckles. "I will gladly fix the issue I created." She took a deep, calming breath before she continued. "And I don't need HIM to do it," she said, nodding her head in Mayan's direction.

Mayan cleared his throat. "I'm sure she needs someone to help her. But I'm not that guy, Geo." Mayan shifted uncomfortably in his chair. "No disrespect, but she's a pain in my ass, and working together is off the table."

Need someone? I don't need anyone!" Gianna huffed loudly. "Like I would ever want to work with you. I can't even count how many times I've thought about shooting you." She put a finger between her eyes. "Right. Fucking. Here, you good for nothing, piece of shit nobody."

"I'll fuckin' gut you like a fish, putana!"

Giovanni stood behind his desk and yelled, spittle flying from his mouth. "WHOA WHOA!" Wincing, he grasped the desk and slowly lowered himself into the big brown leather chair.

He ran his hand through his hair, smoothing it back as he took shaky deep breaths.

"Principessa, I've raised you to be the strongest and most ruthless version of yourself you can be. But, it's no secret that I've done the same for my Principe." He looked at Mayan and his eyes softened. "You might have come from nothing, but you took life by the balls, kid. You're strong and vicious, and you live in the moment."

He shifted his gaze to Gianna. "You're smarter and downright savage. More level-headed; you think more to the future." His eyes closed, and he took a deep breath. Opening his eyes again, he spoke softer than either had ever heard. "Understand that you both need to do this. This fucker thinks he can turn on us? Naw. Never gonna happen."

He took a long drag of his cigar before continuing, seeming to debate his next words. "Your abilities complement each other. Divided, you are strong, but together you are invincible. Let's see what comes of this." His face turned to stone, and his tone went harsh as he said, "I need you both to handle this. No one leaves the life, ever." he said with finality.

Hearing her father refer to Mayan in that way caused her blood to run cold. *You raised me to be ruthless,* she thought before she spoke.

"No one except Roman," she said with a smirk as she crossed her arms and looked directly at Mayan. Excitement coursed through her when he no longer lounged in his chair. His entire body shot up, and his face went flat when he whipped his head in her direction.

"Don't. Don't bring my brother into this, you-" Giovani raised his hands and shouted, "HEY, HEY!" Both his subordinate's heads turned to him, and their mouths shut. "Roman isn't out; he's…" he tilted his head in thought and rubbed his chin. "He has a special set of skills that make it so he isn't required to participate in everyday affairs." His eyes went cold, and he took his cigar from his mouth and pointed it at Gianna. "How do you think we found your man?"

Is he fuckin serious right now? Not only does he protect Mayan but also Roman. Why? What makes them so important? Giovanni continued while she wondered.

"Plus, Roman will be helping pay back his favor in another way."

Mayan's brow furrowed, and he leaned forward. "What? I thought I already paid that debt, Geo."

There was a gleam in his eyes, and a devilish grin spread on his face. "Come on, Mayan. You know better than that."

He slammed his fist down on the desk, and his voice filled the room. "I say when your fuckin' debt is paid!" Mayan sat back in his chair, and Gianna smirked triumphantly. *There he is… That's the Papa I know. You want to play the son, Mayan? Then deal with what I have to live with.* He took a long drag of his cigar before saying,

"You and Gianna will drive to Vegas, where Roman says that little shit is staying. Roman and his girly friend have already been there for a few days. They are waiting for you and Gianna to meet them for a fun getaway.

I bought you three days before the feds get him." He sat back and stared at the man and woman, who had obvious looks of shock on their faces. "I'm not asking. I'm telling. Now get the fuck out of my office." He turned his attention back to his paperwork and waved his hand towards the door.

Gianna took her phone out of her pocket and hurriedly texted before rising from her seat and walking to the door. Ralphy moved swiftly to open it for her with a nod of his head. She stood in the doorway and waited for Mayan's phone to buzz. The corner of her lips tipped up, and her eyes glittered with mischief. He took his phone out as he stood.

"Everything will be taken care of," he said as he turned to the door and looked down at his phone.

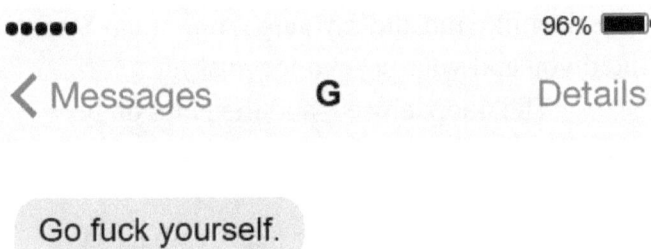

••••• 96% ▰

‹ Messages **G** Details

Go fuck yourself.

Gianna saw Mayan's smile spread before she turned, her wavy hair swishing around her shoulders while she left the room. *That's right— heel boy. If I have to bring you with then you'll be following me,* she thought with delight as she heard his quickened steps approaching.

"Think you're real fuckin' cute, don't you?" he said from behind her.

Looking to the ceiling as she walked, she laughed heartily. "Oh, please. I'm more than cute, and you know it. Is that the game you spit at those little girls you play with from the club? It's pathetic, you know." Gianna pressed the call button for the elevator and stood tapping her toe impatiently as Mayan caught up to her. His ordinarily calm demeanor was off as he hurried, a thick vein in his neck pumped beneath his black tattoos.

She could see that her comment had him heated, and she was loving it.

The elevator doors opened, and as they both stepped in, his voice was cold and low, "I'm sure they like me and my game more than Stefan liked you and your psycho ice pussy."

The doors closed, and the hairs on her arms stood on end as the elevator began its descent.

She mumbled under her breath as she crossed her arms over her chest. "Low blow, cock sock." *He can't hurt you. No one can,* she thought while adding another layer of brick and mortar around her heart.

With a straight face, a shut mouth, and a stiff back, Gianna completed the elevator ride and walked to her car without a glance in his direction. *He's a nobody. Always has been, and always will be.* Gianna knew without a doubt that he was the most insufferable person she had ever met.

As she sat in the leather bucket seat, she pushed her hair from her face and looked into her own eyes in the rearview mirror. "If Papa wasn't so fuckin' snowed by him, I would have already painted the sidewalk with his fuckin' brains," she said, holding her finger to her head and pretending to pull the trigger.

She sat back and started the car, and her text tone rang in sync with the engine starting. She turned it over and opened the text.

Don't say stupid shit anymore, G. I'll be outside your apartment at eight.

Bright light from the screen of her phone illuminated her scrunched face as she lay in her luxurious four-post king-size bed, stretching her naked body out.

She never felt anything but happy when she had her entire bed to herself. Anyone who saw her simple room inevitably asked why she would have such a big bed for one person. She would always smile knowingly and change the subject. She always envisioned herself as a king, not some side-seat ruler like a queen.

●●●●   53% 🔋

< Messages   **Seppie**   Details

> I know you're pissed. But he's not wrong. It's a better cover to have you go down with Mayan and Roman. Plus, with Mayan there, you'll have someone with you in case you run into trouble.

> I don't need anyone. And you should have heard the shit he said about Mayan. He actually called him Principe! I almost threw up.

Whoa, calm down. I do what I do out of love and loyalty. And I wouldn't want any spot in the outfit or our family besides the one I have

If anyone was Principe, it should be YOU! You do so much for that man and our family.

Cugina. Do me a favor. Think about what your dad said. Think of it from his perspective. I know he seems heartless. BUT. You and him are cut from the same cloth. He won't always be here to guide you, and he's trying to prepare you and maybe set you up with a man that might be able to handle your crazy ass. I know I would try to for my daughter.

‹ Messages   **Seppie**   Details

> That's a big bag of flaming shit, Seppie. You know I can't stand that motherfucker. I would NEVER! I can't believe you, and ESPECIALLY my father would say shit like that.

> I'm done with this conversation. I love you. Tell the family I love them, too. I'll text you tomorrow.

Setting her phone down on her single steel side table, Gianna turned off the small Edison bulb lamp and rolled back onto her back, letting her arms spread wide with an exaggerated exhale.

"Stefan left… That's not my fault. He knew who and what I was before we started dating." Her mind went back to the last night she saw him.

She could still remember him standing there in his stupid pink polo shirt and khakis. When she closed her eyes, she saw his sickly white face again. She walked into her apartment with a plastic shopping bag full of hands and teeth.

He had been waiting there to surprise her with dinner and wine. She didn't even think when she plopped the bag in the ceramic kitchen sink, saying, "Hey, I didn't expect you. I was just stopping into shower and didn't want that shit leaking all over my car." After she had tried to kiss him, and he hadn't kissed her back, she realized her mistake. He was in the Outfit but as a numbers guy. Not a killer like her. His stuttering replayed in her mind.

"I. I. I. I. I have to g-g-go."

I should have talked him down. I should have asked him to stay and made him feel better. But she knew she hadn't done any of that because she didn't give a shit about him. She had simply shrugged her shoulders and went to take a shower before she went back out to get rid of the identifiers.

Gianna's lip curled and she hissed into the night.

"His weakness was disgusting." Gianna took comfort in the darkness. Where she belonged, as she said, "I'm doing him a favor by ending his life while I'm down there. For what he did to my reputation because of his lack of balls. I should keep him alive for a week while I let rats feast on his flesh."

Pulling her rich red comforter up, she lay diagonally in her bed and closed her eyes. Gianna's heart-shaped lips continued to smile as she drifted into a dream world filled with cracking screams and bloody streams.

Squealing tires of a shiny, black lotus skidded to a stop before Gianna's tapping pink steel stiletto. She glared down at her large silver watch and huffed in annoyance. When she looked up, she couldn't help but notice him taking her in. *Please, it's not like I wore this for you. Pig.* She thought while looking down at her clothes.

It's summer, and the heat isn't anything to play with. She had chosen tight, short jean shorts and a low-cut white spaghetti strap tank top. She was going to be sitting in a car for hours; the only reason she wore heels was because she always did. Being five-three around towering men wasn't the best way to intimidate them.

"Be ready at eight? It's fuckin' eight twenty."

Never mind the fact that she had waited until eight-ten to come down. Bastard. She wanted to make him wait. Gianna looked into the open passenger window. "So, I'm going to say I'm on my own with putting my bag in the car, huh?" She rolled her eyes at Mayan's wide grin.

"Oh, I'm sorry, G. I thought you were all big bad woman. But I guess if you need me to carry your little bag for you, I can," he said, grabbing the door handle.

Gianna sneered and pulled up her rolling bag by the handle and threw it through the window at him. "Don't bother; I wouldn't want you to hurt yourself, sweetie."

Mayan threw his hands up to block his face. "Fuck G!" He yelled as the hard plastic of the luggage banged into his arms.

There was no hiding the smile on her face as she opened the door and sat while he shoved it into the back seat.

He shook his head and groaned. "Great, this is going to be a long ride," he grumbled while pulling away from the curb and into the steady flow of cars.

Two hours of playing on her phone, avoiding the idiot next to her was all she could take.

"Stop off at the next exit," she said curtly.

Mayan's eyes shot to her. "Oh yes, ma'am. Right away, ma'am." he chuckled while passing the exit and looked her in the eyes. "I'm not stopping until you say please, you little brat."

Gianna smiled defiantly. "If you won't stop… I'll just piss on your seat."

His face curled in disgust. "Fuckin' gross G. Can't you just say please?"

"…Please, stop at the next exit." She said with an innocent smile while batting her eyes. Then, she promptly stuck her tongue out at him and sat back, crossing her arms.

Mayan stopped at the best-looking gas station, and Gianna hurried out to the washroom while Mayan talked to himself and began to fill the tank. "Might as well since we are stopped."

After peeing from an impressive distance from the more than questionable toilet seat, Gianna walked out of the gas station. The bells hanging from the top rang loudly as she noticed he wasn't in the car, so she scanned the parking lot for Mayan.

"Great. Where did he go?" She began to turn in a circle, but before she could complete it, she turned right into Mayan, bumping her bare chest against his exposed arms. "Oh, I'm sorry," she said, stepping back with heat rising in her cheeks. She couldn't remember the last time they had touched one another. With the blush shining bright, she turned, went straight for the car, and got in. Grabbing her phone to avoid looking at him, she sent off a text to Seppie.

●●   37% 🔋

❮ Messages   **Seppie**   Details

> This is fuckin' awful! How many more hours do I have of this?!

OMG, get over it, ya big baby. How hard can it be to sit in a car?

A crinkling bag of potato chips pushed into her arm as Mayan set down his arm full of junk food.

He pulled out his phone, and as he read, she watched his jaw tighten. Flinging the phone into the cup holder, he started the car and pulled out of the gas station. "I'm not stopping again for a while, so I hope you got something while you were in there."

She looked down at the giant stash of candy, chips, and pop and laughed loudly. "Seriously, you look like a kid with a twenty."

"What? I like to snack. If you want to worry about your girlish figure, you go right ahead. But don't judge me." he said playfully while pulling back out onto I-80.

She shook her head. "It reminds me of you and Roman when we were younger." She picked up a bag of skittles. "Look, you even got his favorite." Mayan's smile fell, and his body became rigid. She looked at him curiously. "I've wondered what happened between you and him?" Mayan's only response was to reach forward and turn the radio on. She spoke louder, "Seriously, Mayan, I'm not trying…" Mayan continued to turn the volume up as she talked until the music drowned her out.

Oh fuck no! Who the hell does this mother fucker think he is? I was trying to pretend like we were normal! Gianna's face was red with anger, and her entire body was tense. |

"I'm no chump ass bitch, Mayan!" She screamed while removing her shoe and slamming the pointed steel heel into the display screen of the radio.

Mayan swerved to the side of the road and squealed to a stop, pushing the button to his hazard lights. Gianna's chest was heaving with rage as he stared at her with his mouth agape.

Finally able to form words Mayan spit out. "What the actual fuck G!" he pointed to his radio. "Are you fucking kidding me? You want to know that goddamn bad?!" Suddenly, a look of pain spread across his face, and he looked down at the bag of skittles. For a moment, she was reminded that she had a heart.

"I don't know, G. Your guess is as good as mine. Maybe I'll ask him while we are there dealing with your fuckin' mistake." The pain left his face, and anger took over as he turned to look her in the eyes. "But that's none of your damn business, it hasn't been since you decided you didn't need us."

And just like that, with that little speech, Gianna's heart was locked away once again.

"Just drive. I'll pay for the radio when we get there." She said, pulling her heel from it. Mayan didn't respond; he turned off the hazards and pulled back onto the highway. She picked up her phone and was about to text Seppie all about the dumbass she was being forced to work with when a bag of Sour Patch Kids landed hard in her lap

"I got your favorite too."

It took Gianna two more bathroom breaks and a stop in a fast-food drive-through to get the lump out of her throat and finally say more than yes and no to him.

Hell, after a total of six and a half hours in the car and more than one uncomfortable interaction, she was pretty much ready to fight a bear to get into a nice hotel.

My ass hurts, and I'm ready for a bowl and a relaxing bath, she thought as the cool night air splashed across her face through the window.

"Hey, umm…" She cleared her throat before continuing. "Did you have a hotel in mind? It's getting pretty late."

Mayan looked at her briefly. "No, no. We are going to go as long as we can, maybe take a nap at a truck stop."

Gianna's eyes went wide, and her mouth hung open for a full five seconds. "For real?" He nodded. "Absolutely not going to happen," she said, shaking her head and waving her hands. "What do you think I am? Some homeless chick?" She picked up her phone and started typing furiously. "I looked up hotels before we left." She flashed the screen at him. "Look, this one is only thirty minutes away, AND they have whirlpool baths and room service."

Mayan rolled his eyes but continued to look at the road ahead. "Fine. Put the GPS on and I'll take you there, so you'll shut the fuck up." Her mouth opened, but her words caught in her throat when his striking green eyes fell on her. He quirked an eyebrow and purred, "Princess."

Twenty-five minutes later, Mayan and Gianna walked into the Starlight Hotel.

"Told ya I would beat the GPS." His white smile gleamed confidently as he strode to the front desk, where a man with short brown hair and a welcoming smile stood. She made a dumb face at the back of his head *like I ever said you wouldn't. Men are so damn weird.*

Mayan greeted the man respectfully as he approached the desk. "Hi, we don't have reservations. But would you happen to have any rooms available?"

Tapping his fingers on the keyboard while Mayan spoke, he quickly answered. "Hi, I'm Scott. We can definitely accommodate you." He looked between them and the computer. We have a queen-size bed in a standard suite and a king-size bed in a presidential suite." He set his hands on the desk and smiled. "Which one would you two prefer?"

Looking between each other and the man, their eyes bulged in disbelief.

Mayan laughed. "Us?" He pointed between himself and Gianna. "Never. We need two rooms."

"I'll take the king," Gianna said firmly.

Mayan huffed. "Why do you get the king?"

Gianna took the card key, "Thank you so much, Scott." She turned to Mayan, flipping her long dark hair over her shoulder. "Because you're more of a bitch than me, so naturally, you require a queen." His eyebrow raised at her remark, and she knew she had gotten under his skin.

"I'm sure you can handle the bill, big boy." She gave him a cute wink and a pat on the shoulder, then walked past him to the elevator. His deep chuckle conjured goosebumps on her skin as she pressed the call button.

She stepped into the elevator and rubbed at her arm as though she could push the bumps back into her skin as the doors closed. The mirrored elevator jumped to life and she jerked forward. Her eyes met her dark gaze in the reflection as she leaned back against the wall. "I hate his fuckin' crooked ass grin and that laugh…" She groaned while she glared at herself. "Why do you let him affect you? You know who he is and what he's done." She looked down at her shoes, unable to look at herself, while she said, "Never forget."

Her body swayed forward as the elevator stopped and the doors glided open. Stepping out, Gianna strolled to her room. Within seconds, she found her door. Placing the key card before the scanner, she pressed down on the golden handle.

She pushed the door open to her suite, and her shoulders relaxed at the welcoming sight.

Standing before her was a beautifully made king-size bed with all white linen. With an audible sigh of relief, she walked in and kicked her shoes off. After she threw her bag onto the bed, she headed to the bathroom.

Reaching in past the open door, she found the switch on the wall and flicked the lights on. She let out a deep exhale and looked longingly at the large white whirlpool tub.

"Oh, thank god." She rolled her eyes. "Pfft… And he wanted me to stay in the car at a truck stop." Spinning back toward the room on her tiptoes, she proclaimed, "Boy, must be out his damn mind!"

Excited, she went to her bag like a kid who had found the Halloween candy stash. Unzipping it, she removed her deep purple silk nighty, rainbow sherbert cart, and toiletries and then returned to the bathroom. *Non-smoking room.* Gianna rolled her eyes at the 'rule.' *Catch me first,* she thought with a smirk, then took a long, drawn-out hit, enjoying the feeling of the cool smoke filling her lungs.

After setting up the soaps and hair products she always bought from the poshest salon in town, she stripped and began to fill the bath.

"Oh, fuck, I should have room service bring up a bottle and something to snack on."

She turned from the tub and held her bare breasts as she ran on tiptoe to the phone to call down for some wine and cheese.

Bouncing from foot to foot, she read the list of numbers pinned next to the phone. "There it is!" She picked up the receiver and dialed zero-zero.

A young woman promptly answered the call within two rings. "Room Service, this is Emily speaking. I see you're in room three twenty-seven. Can I have something brought up for you?"

"Hi, would it be possible to bring up a bottle of sweet red wine and perhaps a tray of cheeses?"

"Absolutely, ma'am, anything else?"

"No, that will be all." Gianna's head tilted, and a smirk appeared. "That gets charged to the credit card on file, correct?"

"Precisely."

A twinkle of playful joy zipped through her. "Amazing, make sure it's the most expensive bottle. And leave a fifty-dollar tip for me."

"I'll get right on that. Someone will be up with your order within the next half hour. We hope you are enjoying your stay."

"I am. Thank you so much." As she hung up, her eyes landed on the bag of Sour Patch Kids. *Room service is going to take a minute.* She scooped them up and flopped back on the comfy bed.

Instead of eating them, though, she raised them above her face and fiddled with the bag. *I don't think Stefan even knew I liked candy. Let alone my favorite kind.* Her heart pounded on the brick encasing it, causing little fissures to appear. Without realizing it, she began to drift into the past when it all began. She had only met them because Roman was involved with her father. Gianna had never made friends easily. Roman saw her when no one else did. He brought her into their little circle. Giving her people she thought she could call her own.

She remembered Mayan walking out of a corner store with his pockets full of candy he had stolen for them all to share. *How did Roman and Mayan drift so far apart?* In her mind, she saw Roman at fifteen. He used to be so fun and full of life. Free. A sneer marred her face. *That was before SHE got ahold of him and beat him into submission.*

Shaking her head clear of that awful bitch, she returned to reminiscing.

She returned to Roman, slinging an arm around an eleven-year-old version of Mayan with a wide smile as Mayan handed him a bag of Skittles. "Good job, kid, but be careful. Candy ain't worth juvie." *He was always so proud and protective of him.*

She smiled wistfully, recalling how ridiculous Nickels looked at eight, ripping into a giant laughy-taffy with his buck teeth. Her head began to shake, and a tiny laugh escaped her.

Dante never stopped yelling at Nickels. "If you rip those big ass teeth out of your head eating crap like that, don't come running to me." But then again, he yelled at everyone. He was always the mama hen of the group.

She had gotten so lost in the past that when a knock sounded on the door, she shot up. Her hand instinctively slid under the pillow in search of the cold metal of her tiny beretta bobcat she never slept without. Reminding herself that she literally asked someone to come to her room, she slid off the bed.

She stood there naked for a second and shook her hands and head, attempting to get the crazy off. *Maybe you don't need the wine; that weed seems to be doing well enough on its own.*

Another knock at the door had her out of her thoughts and walking to the washroom to grab the first towel she saw and toss the candy on the side of the tub.

She yelled to the impatient visitor as she wrapped the towel around herself. "Hold on. I'll be right there." Tucking the towel into itself, she looked down at her almost visible crotch. "Fucking great. I have to ask for better towels." She shrugged and laughed as she walked to the door. "With a towel like this, he better not ask for a tip."

Pushing down the gold handle with one hand and ensuring her towel was secure with the other, she opened the door. Her brows knit together, and her mouth opened with no words forthcoming at first. She just stared at the man holding the wine and cheese. "Mayan?"

The corner of his lips tipped up, and her heart jumped. "Yeah, I saw some guy coming to your room. I thought it would be better if I took everything from him and gave it to you." His eyes narrowed, and he looked down both sides of the hall jokingly. "Lord only knows what kind of weirdos live out here in Nebraska." He handed her the covered plate, bottle, and a single long-stem wine glass.

She looked down at the bottle and thought of how sweet it was going to feel, sweeping past her dry lips to caress her cotton mouth with its velvet liquid. "Umm, Thanks. I think." She said incredulously while licking her lips.

Looking up, she was caught off guard. His bright green eyes were fixed on her lips. She had wandered into the trap and was caught by the entrancing sparkle. Unable to break away from his eyes, she followed as they drifted down her body and lingered on her hand holding the bottle. Right in front of the itty-bitty darkened opening in the front of her tiny towel.

Her cheeks heated, and she felt her body respond to his unwavering gaze. "Okay," she said awkwardly while looking anywhere but at him. "I'm going inside now. Have a good night," she said as she began to shut the door. His eyes stayed glued in place as his scarred hand grabbed the edge of the door and pushed, keeping her from closing it.

His intense stare and forceful action stirred the deep pool of passion within her. And for one astonishingly insane second, she considered dropping the towel. Her grip began to loosen of its own accord.

Then, without warning, his face hardened, and his eyes met hers.

"Don't open the door again tonight. I'll see you in the morning." She stood there staring at him as he turned and began to walk away. She begged her mind. *Something. Say something. Anything. Don't just stand here.*

The only thing her clambaked brain could manage to sputter out was, "Thank you... For the sour patch kids."

She watched in horror as he stopped, and his body tensed. Before he could turn, she closed the door. She stood there. Staring at the door blankly for a second, and then the wheels in her brain began to turn.

Anger began to build, and she stomped to the bathroom. *Why was he watching my door? Probably to 'protect' me again,* she thought angrily while setting up the final touches of her bath.

The scratchy terry cloth towel dropped to the floor, pooling around her white tip-manicured feet before she stepped into the pampering bath. Slowly submerging her body, she savored every second of her muscles loosening one by one. The water rose to her shoulders, covering her slender, curvy body entirely. Gianna's wet fingers curled around the cool glass of wine. Bringing the glass to her lips, she held it tipped, allowing the sweet red wine to splash against her heated lips.

If she could have stopped her mind, she would have. But the past refused to die as her eyes landed on the innocent bag of candy.

Her eyes closed tight in an attempt to hide from it all, and she was instantly transported to the past.
The past, she had worked so hard to outrun all these years.

She was sixteen. Her light blue shirt stuck to her sweaty skin, and she rubbed her clammy hands on her tight blue jeans. Her eyes darted from side to side, surveying the narrow alleyway for a way around the four imposing boys. Leon, Tommy, Charles, and Jose towered over her, even in their juvenile forms.

"You guys said the coke deal was good. I buy it off you and then give it to a crew to distribute. If the deal isn't good anymore, I can take my money elsewhere, tons of lowlife drug dealers in the city." She said bravely as her voice quavered.

Jose stepped toward her, and she tried to take two back but was met by a dumpster at her back. *When did they corner me?? Idiota! You know better,* she thought, running her hands on the cold metal.

"That's not nice, G. You know, you don't have to hurt my feelings," Jose said, turning his lips down into a mocking frown.

"It's not personal, G."

Leon's soft voice came from behind Jose. "It's your dad G. He found out you were messing around in this shit."

Gianna's entire body went as cold as ice, the hairs on her neck standing on end. *FUCK FUCK FUCK!* She screamed in her mind. Attempting to brave through the shock, she cockily said, "And? So you should know better than to fuck with me then."

Jose shook his head and smiled. "That's the thing, G. He paid us more than what you were going to, AND we got to keep our supply." He brought his hands together and rubbed his knuckles.

Before she could register what was happening, Jose's fist was crashing into her nose, and a streak of lightning shot through her head before it slammed back into the unforgiving metal of the dumpster. Blood gushed from her nose, and hot tears spilled down her cheeks.

Jose squatted before her, putting his finger under her chin to make her raise her eyes to his. They were cold, and there was not a trace of the friendship she had thought they had. "He told me to teach you a lesson. Never trust anyone and stay away from the shit your father tells you to."

Jose's hand cocked back again, and Gianna clenched her eyes closed, readying for another hit; *nothing he could do would hurt more than Papa sending them to do this.* Her gut turned at the thought, the pain worse than the radiating pain in her face and head.

Gianna's eyes sprang open when she heard a booming voice yell, "Get the fuck away from her!"

"Mayan!" Her heart was racing, but with Jose distracted, she swung her fist into his face. His head flung to the side, and the rest of his body followed. As he toppled over, Gianna jumped to her feet. She pushed past the gaping boys with their hands in the air and right into Mayan's arms, smearing blood all over his shirt when she hid her face in his broad chest.

Safely in Mayan's arms, she heard Roman call out, "Don't fuckin' move, Jose. Put your fuckin' hands up."

Hot breath fanned her ear, "Run," Mayan whispered as he flung her behind him.

Gianna's feet carried her as far away from them as she could get. She could never have known just how far away from Mayan she was destined to go.

Chapter 5. Principe Demone

His Past. And their future?

"Thanks… For the sour patch kids." Every muscle in Mayan's body tensed, and he froze in place. After seeing her in her towel, with her dark hair tossed and disheveled, and her plump lips wet from her sinful tongue. Hearing those words fall from her mouth was unfair. The ice princess thanking him as though she didn't hate the air he breathed was almost too much. It took every bit of restraint to keep himself from turning around and pushing her into the room.

Fuck the food and wine; I'll show her just how thankful she can be while I take every bit of her. His fists clenched, and the door clicked shut. *Good.* Even after the door closed, Mayan stood there in the hallway, staring at the deep red carpet, trying to calm the savage beast within him.

It doesn't mean anything to her. Nothing I do does. Hasn't in years. He shook those thoughts from his mind. *And more importantly. I don't care.*

He lifted his chin confidently and began to walk. As he attempted to walk casually to his room, his mind continued to tell his heart and dick reasons he needed to walk away.

It was the same old song and dance. His mind never cared how much it killed his heart when it was reminded why Mayan hated Gianna La Rosa.

His hand raised to his chest, and he began to scratch at the old scar. *I should have gotten a thank you when I saved her*. He pushed his fingertips into his shirt harder. The raised ridges of the deeply ruined skin caught on his nails as he scraped them across his chest. Pain overtook the pleasurable sensation of scratching the itch, and his teeth ground together with a hiss. *Instead, I got this*.

He tore his hand from his chest before he could break the skin. Like he did every other time he thought about that disaster. Shoving his hands in his pockets, he quickened his steps and made it to his room. Unfortunately, after his run-in with G, the low lighting of the hotel hallway and the burning itch on his chest created the perfect storm. Turning the handle to his room, he was suddenly transported back to the old warehouse. He could feel everything like he was truly there right now.

His skin was slick with sweat from the summer heat, making his black tank top cling to his bronzed skin. He fidgeted with it while he walked into the office, Roman lazily trailing behind him.

The loud click of the hotel door shutting behind him brought him back from the unwanted trip down memory lane. Mayan pulled his white v-neck shirt over his broad shoulders and tossed it to the floor.

As much as he wanted to let this go and forget about what just happened, he knew he wouldn't. He couldn't help it; his heart wanted so badly to push back against his brain. Against everything that was factual and logical. He shook his head, attempting to clear his mind as he fell back into the bed. *Queen-size bed,* he thought as he placed his hands behind his head. "More of a bitch than her." A chuckle escaped him. "No one is more of a bitch than her."

His primal side was never willing to stay quiet for long. Especially when Gianna was involved, *I could be sinking into a princess right now.* The thought of G in her tiny hotel towel filled his mind and hardened his cock, his tongue sliding across his plump lips.

He smacked his hands hard against his face. The sudden stinging sensation helped to lessen the pressure of his erection against the zipper of his tight, dark blue jeans. Sliding his hands up his face, he fisted his hair and growled.

"Stop! You stupid motherfucker! There are a million bitches out there. All of them warmer than that freezer."

Closing his eyes, his heart filled with an all-too-familiar rage. His mind was once again reminding his heart why it had to stay locked away. Suddenly, he was seventeen again, and the stale smoke-filled air stung his nose as he entered the warehouse office.

A younger, leaner Ralphy sat behind the desk, not acknowledging the pair as they entered. He tapped the long ash of his cigarette against the ashtray. There was about a pack or more of cigarette butts already overflowing it. *Tough day,* Mayan thought, while he took the only available chair. As he sat, the chain that connected his wallet to his pants clanged against the rolling chair, filling the quiet office.

It had taken him longer than it should have to see that something was off. Before the words could leave his mouth, Roman spoke from the doorway. "What's wrong, Ralphy?"

Mayan's mouth tightened. His older brother was always one step ahead of him, even when he was behind him. Ralphy's full head of black curls bounced as he shook his head, refusing to look up from the scared desk.

Mayan's voice was small, "Ralphy?" He had never seen the stone man so solemn.

"I can't."

"What do you mean you can't, Ralphy?"

Mayan demanded, his body becoming rigid with anxiety.

"Fuck, Mayan, I can't tell anyone, especially you," he said, covering his eyes with his hands as he leaned back in his chair and groaned.

Mayan made to stand, but Roman placed a hand on his shoulder to keep him seated. *When did he come up next to me?* He thought, pushing the hand from his shoulder with a sneer.

Ralphy dropped his hands from his face and brought his eyes down to finally look at the boys, First Roman and then Mayan.

Shaking his head, he finally spoke, "I shouldn't, but I can't. He's wrong. Teresa would never allow this if she knew." His eyes grew sad. "Geo found out Gianna was trying to deal in drugs." Mayan didn't need anyone to tell him how bad that was.

Roman looked down at his feet, not saying anything in return.

"What, what does that mean?" Mayan asked, his voice raising loud enough that Roman looked at him. "I get that, that's bad. But why? What's he going to do to her? She's a little old for a spanking."

"He's going to teach her a lesson."

Roman swore under his breath, "Fuck."

Mayan screamed while standing up and slamming his hands down on the desk, "Clearly, I'm fuckin' missing something. What the fuck is going on?!"

Ralphy shot up, leaning over the desk enough that he was only about an inch from Mayans face when he bellowed, "He set her up! She's going to get her shit rocked! She'll be lucky if she walks out of there by herself." Falling back to the seat, Mayan's blood froze into rivers of slush.

"She knows the group she set the deal up with, though," Roman said.

"She does. But so does Geo, and his pockets are deeper. Even deeper when he's pissed." Ralphy's face seemed to pale. "And he is fuckin' livid; I've never seen him this way."

Having heard all he cared to, Mayan stood abruptly, slamming the chair back into the office's dingy white cinder block wall, and stalked to the door.

He wasn't about to let anyone hurt her. As he passed over the threshold, a strong hand grabbed his shoulder and jerked him back. He came to a dead stop before ripping himself free and spinning on his brother.

"What?" He yelled, spraying spittle out that almost hit Roman's face. "You can't stop me. I won't let anyone hurt her!"

Roman shook his head, and a small smile curved the corner of his lips. Lifting the bottom of his shirt, Roman revealed a nine-mm handgun shoved into the waist of his pants.

"No one is going to hurt her," he said with finality while jerking his head toward the hallway. Mayan clasped his brother's shoulder and weakly smiled. He knew he didn't need to say thank you. He knew Roman understood the silent language that bonded brothers held.

As the two boys strode down the hall, determined to save the damsel in distress, they heard Ralphy's voice echo off the walls.

"Don't you fuckin' let those low-life mother fuckers hurt her."

Rushing out into the bright summer sun, Mayan swung open the door to Roman's shitty

Geo metro, and slid in. Coincidentally, it was the only car he ever remembered his brother owning.

He growled as he rolled over to his stomach. "Fuck Roman. He's no better than her. I didn't do anything to deserve him avoiding me like the damn plague."

Ready to escape the world and his memories, Mayan closed his tired eyes and allowed sleep to take him.

**No one can run from their own mind…
Especially while they sleep.**

Crushing hands wrenched back Mayan's young, scrawny, muscled teenage arms with bruising force, making it impossible to protect himself.

Searing pain lanced through his bare chest, and thick, wet blood poured down, pooling around his feet and becoming deep red bricks, encasing his feet. The knife began pulling from his chest, and it went on and on like a clown with a hanky. When it eventually slid out of his chest, his head lulled in exhaustion.

Finally, having enough strength, Mayan attempted to raise his head to speak, only to be met with a claw-spiked hand the size of a frying pan connecting with his face.

The world around him shuttered with the impact and became stained red.

His knees buckled beneath him. Looking at the legs that had betrayed him, he found that he now possessed the legs of a colt.

They were weak and wobbly, unable to carry him through the world.

Eyes like black wading pools stared into his as the giant assaulting him slithered a slimy blue serpent tongue into his ear. It swirled down until it reached his brain and began tickling it. Sliding past, it exited out through his tear duct and swiped over his eye, stealing his tears, before retreating back to the dripping grotesque mouth it came from.

Sticky drool slid down his slumped shoulders as the giant whispered, its voice a grave rumble.

"You shouldn't have interfered with me teaching my Principessa a lesson."

Setting the cold, gleaming knife on his raw chest, the giant moved to stare into Mayan's soul. "Tell me who told you!" he demanded.

Mayan feebly shook his swollen head. "No one. I figured it out on my own. I made Roman come with." His voice came out as tiny mouse squeaks, but he continued. "He had the gun. I needed him."

Mayan's head began to sting with pricks of pain as a crown of barbed wire rose up from beneath his skin, popping the skin on his forehead open. Bright yellow blood started running into his eyes, obscuring his vision.

The giant's wet lips slowly spread into a smile, revealing his three rows of tiny, sharp piranha teeth. His smile grew, extending past his face.

He slowly sank the knife deep, proclaiming, "Let this be a lesson to you, Principe. This thing... is going to get you in trouble."

The giant's open mouth widened as it unhinged its jaw. The disgusting tongue slid out again. This time, it didn't assault him. It flicked and waved in the air. As it did, streams of goo fell from it, turning to black smoke before hitting the ground. The rancid smoke didn't disperse. Instead, it encased him, flowing into his mouth and nose.

He felt it invading his lungs and filling them until his chest expanded. It continued to painfully expand until he felt his lungs burst with a pop, leaving him no way to take a breath. His chest collapsed, and his mouth hung open with no sound. His throat spasmed wildly as he tried desperately to breathe.

The smoke, now as thick as wool, pushed in on his already concave chest like a bug between fingers. The smoke continued to push and slide, smearing him until he was something that needed to be wiped away from the world.

A loud snapping sound shook the world, and the smoke cleared. He plummeted to the ground, smashing hard against it.

Fighting through the pain, he rose, standing with his back straight and chin raised. He was now a full-grown man, unhindered and unable to cry, his tears having been stolen, a treasure the giant now held.

They were now a shining blue gem hanging around the monster's fat neck. Not a single muscle on him twitched as the giant completed the dripping deep X on his chest.

Looking into those black pools, Mayan smiled. "Thank you."

Waking from his nightmare, he sat up abruptly, his eyes searching the room wildly. A coating of sweat covered his skin, and his breaths were ragged and uneven as he clutched at the old nightmare-inducing scar.

The bright light of the early morning streaming in through the windshield stung Mayan's tired eyes as he sent the text.

●●●●   100% ▬

‹ Messages   **G**   Details

> I'm in the car. Whether you're in here or not, I'm leaving in thirty minutes.

I'll do as I damn well please. And you know it! You'll wait, or I'll slit your nut sack open and wear your little balls as earrings.

Beautiful, straight, white teeth showed as Mayan's smile took over his face. Sitting in the tiny gas station parking lot across the street from the hotel, he chuckled while watching G exit the front door. Her face instantly went red, and her head swiveled from side to side before she dropped the handle to her bag. With a stomp of her tiny foot, she pulled out her phone. Mayan's eyes twinkled with anticipation at the sight.

Where the fuck are you?!

After reading her text, one eyebrow popped up with the corner of his mouth as he sent…

> You're an entitled little brat! I told you thirty minutes… It's been forty-five bitch.

The following text had Mayan looking up, with a look of surprise marring his beautiful features.

> You're so fucking dumb!!! LOL! I can see that flashy ass lotus in the sea of fords! XD

His eyes narrowed to slits as he watched her put her middle finger up, then turn her wrist until the offending finger was pointing to the ground before the haughty bitch.

> Heel boy ;)

Mayan's mouth turned to a sly smile. *I can't even help myself. This bitch's mouth is going to get her into trouble.*

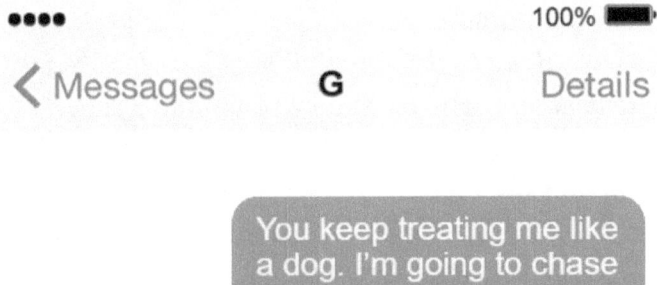

Wetting his lips with a broad swipe of his tongue, Mayan couldn't help but imagine taking a big bite of that scrumptious sopping wet pussy cat with his big bad wolf fangs. It never mattered how hard he tried. How much he told himself and everyone else that he never would. He would always hold a dumb ass flame for that cunt.

Ready for the chase, Mayan shifted the lotus into gear, and the engine roared to life. Peeling out of the parking lot, he zipped around the small onset of traffic and whipped into the half-circle drive, screeching to a stop before her.

His heart nearly tore from his chest as he took her in. Petite black High-top Converse tapped on the cement sidewalk.

A pair of low-rise yoga capris hugged her now
thick hips just as well as they did when they were
young. A white V-neck crop top showed off the
blue gemmed belly button ring and her enticing
hourglass figure.

*What is she doing? What kind of fucked up
game is this?* His face screwed up into a sneer.
*I'm not doing this. Fuck her. I won't give her the
reaction she wants.*

Opening the door, Gianna tossed her bag
into the back and plopped down in the passenger
seat. Unaware or uncaring that he was clearly
upset, she pulled her phone out and quickly filled
the car with the dinging sounds of her newest
game.

Mayans eye began to twitch as the sounds
and her attitude filed down the tiny shred of self-
control he had left, keeping him from exploding.

Without looking up from her game,
Gianna dictated their schedule for the day.

"Okay, so let's stop for breakfast
somewhere first." She waved a hand toward him
absently. "I don't care where; a drive-thru will
work just fine." Returning her hand to the phone,
she continued, "Then we can drive all day and just
grab some shitty gas station food when we fill
up." A loud wah wah wah sounded from her
phone, interrupting her orders. Her face pinched.
"Fuck." Biting on her lip, her fingers began

146

tapping vigorously on the screen.

Pain spiked as Mayan bit down on his tongue that was held at bay between his teeth. The bright taste of copper bloomed in his mouth, giving him something else to focus on.

No reply snuck past his tightly closed lips. Grasping the steering wheel as hard as Jack held the door in the Titanic, he put the car into drive and hurried toward their destination. Inside, he held a slew of curse words and nasty comments. Safely locked away so they didn't shoot or stab one another. Seeing her dressed the way she used to infuriated him. It reminded him of being dumb and ready to lose it all to fall in love for an eternity.

I'm going to fuckin' kill her before lunch, he thought. His eye twitched in response to the loud dings coming from his passenger seat. Rummaging through his stuff, he found his earbuds and looked longingly at his busted radio. *Bitch.*

Contrary to what he thought would happen, Mayan kept his mouth shut for almost the entire day. He used his headphones to ignore G. He committed himself to only small grunts and gestures when he was required to reply in some way.

It had also taken longer than he expected for Gianna to grow tired of his passive-aggressive bitchiness. But she did.

She sat up suddenly, smacking her phone down onto her thigh. "What the fuck is your problem now?"

Mayan's lips thinned to toothpicks. "Nothing."

Gianna's eyes rolled hard, and she huffed loudly before picking her phone back up and lounging in her seat again. "Whatever."

An hour later, it was seven thirty, and he could feel the electricity jumping between them. It was crackling, and soon, she would set it free to wreak havoc. He knew it.

"Listen here, you big bitch! I don't know what the fuck your problem is now, but I'm about to straddle you and strangle the fuck out of you until you tell me."

Mayan's knuckles whitened, and his forearm flexed. The artfully beheaded naked woman tattooed on the back of his arm arched. He spun the wheel toward the oncoming exit and hit the gas.

Out of the corner of his eye, he saw G's head bounce off the window with the sudden turn. Giving him a slight ping of satisfaction that quirked his lips up to a smile; *good. Maybe it knocked some sense into her, talking to me like that.* He made no move to hide his delight.

Gianna hissed while clutching her head.

"What the fuck, Mayan!? Where are you going?"

"Gas station," he said, pulling into the brightly lit gas station and slamming the lotus into park in front of the pump closest to the doors.

Pushing the car door with his foot, he stepped out. Then growled as he slammed it shut behind him, making the entire car shutter. "Just give me a fuckin' minute. I'll be back."

He walked into the shit-hole gas station and quickly realized he had no idea what the hell he was doing there. The tall, polite woman with an impressive five o'clock shadow waved to him with a nod.

Taking another step into the small store, he scanned the wears. He saw a wire rack of dusty snack-sized potato chip bags, a pair of dark shriveled hot dogs rolling slowly on a heater, and some coolers filled with drinks. He ended his perusal on the dirtiest fountain drink dispenser he had ever seen.

He stuck his tongue out and shook his head. "Yuck." And as if a light bulb exploded into fireworks above his head, he suddenly had an idea. *Oh, you want to play games and make me uncomfortable? I'll fix you, you dumb cunt.*

He took out his phone and quickly searched for motels in the area. Giving the bearded Viking a nod, he turned back to the door and walked out, staring at his phone.

He found what he was looking for with a smug smile before getting into the car again.

He had no intention of looking at the medusa of a woman sitting beside him or provoking her, for that matter. With her eyes drilling straight through him and to the earth's center, he started the car and drove.

"Are you ready to tell me what your problem is?" she asked between gritted teeth.

"You're loving this. Aren't you?" he questioned angrily.

"Loving what? You, cryptic freak."

"G, I haven't seen you in anything but heels since we were teenagers."

He looked over to her and gestured to her midsection, catching her body going stiff as a board as he spoke. "And I certainly haven't seen that piercing since…" He put a finger to his chin and mocked deep thought. "Oh, I don't know. I think the last time I saw that little fucker make an appearance; I was making out with you behind a forklift at the old warehouse on forty-seventh St." He could feel his chest rising and falling hard. He was so mad he almost missed his turn.

Gianna sat silently. Too silent. Her nostrils flared, her nails digging deep into the black leather. "Why G? Why would you do that shit?"

He looked at her for just a second. Her eyes were two large obsidian stones, trained on his every movement. His eyes swung back to the road, a feeble attempt at saving what little bit of his soul was left. His voice was quiet now, no bluster or bravado. "You really are that cold. Aren't you?"

Lightning flashed through her eyes, and her mouth opened while she jutted her tiny finger in his direction. "You think you know?" she snarled. "You don't know shit about me." She closed her eyes and took in a few deep breaths, seeming to gather herself.

Before she could speak, the car stopped, and Mayan shifted it into park. Her eyes popped open just in time to see Mayan open the door and rock the car once again as he slammed it behind him. Gravel crunched beneath his pristine white Nike gym shoes as he stomped his way to the dilapidated sea-blue motel and into the cramped office.

He was immediately punched in the face by the worst smell he had ever come across. *Ughhh, B.O. is putting it lightly. Jesus is this what Jerry Seinfeld's car smelled like?*

Walking up to the rotund man in the yellowish-white tank top, Mayan decided he was where the smell was being birthed.

For a smell that smelly did not just exist; it was born of malice. *Maybe picking the closest one-star motel wasn't the best idea*, he thought as he greeted the black-toothed man wielding a fly swatter valiantly.

"Uhh, hello." Mayan stopped for a second while he watched the deceptively graceful man rise from the sad rolling chair and stalk what seemed to be an extremely stealthy fly. "I don't mean to distract you from the hunt or anything... but I need two rooms if you have them."

Tiptoeing towards the fly that had just landed on the wall that Mayan hoped was painted green, the man crouched into a ready position. Two inches of his buttcrack on full display. *Oh sure... I'm sure the crack exposure makes him more aerodynamic.*

Mayan's eyebrow rose to his hairline in bewilderment as he watched the hunter wave the fly swatter to the right of the fly like a ribbon dancer. *Is he trying to kill it or mate with it? Either way, awkwardly enough, I can't look away.*

Suddenly, a loud thwap reverberated through the tiny room, stinging Mayan's ears. His jaw dropped, and the other eyebrow met its twin at the hairline as he watched that fat little guy drag his hand down the wall and then turn his palm over to reveal a splatter.

With an itty-bitty, black-toothed grin, the man placed his palm on his belly and wiped down. "Names Ashley. I got two rooms. Fifty bucks each for the night or ten for the hour," he stated in a frog-like croak.

"Congratulations on the kill, Ashley," Mayan said, jutting his chin toward the man's belly. "I'm Mike. Mike Katowski. Nice to meet ya. I'll take the two best rooms you have and give you one fifty if you make sure the sheets and pillowcases are *actually* clean."

"Why certainly, Your Majesty," the man said with a flourished bow.
"But it's one seventy-five for two clean sheet sets," he said with a wink while tossing two gold keys with red plastic tags onto the sticky counter. The numbers nine and ten were written in gold pen paint.
Trading out the keys for the cash, Mayan pocketed number ten and headed for the door.

"Change out nine first. The lady will be using her room immediately," he ordered as the rickety screen door swung closed behind him.

Looking up from the keys in his hand, Mayan wished he could have kept his mouth shut longer. A black high top came whirling at his face fast enough that it caught him off guard and square on the nose.

"Fuck G!" he screamed, holding his nose. The screen door slammed, and he heard a 'ha-yuck' of a laugh from behind.

"I don't want a shoe to the face. I'll go change the lady's sheets now," Ashley said through bouts of laughter.

"The lady's sheets?" Gianna said incredulously. "I'm not fucking staying here in this roach motel," she proclaimed loudly.

Still holding his nose, Mayan went to the car, pulled her suitcase from it, and tossed it to the ground. "You most certainly are, princess," He said, sliding into the driver's seat and locking the doors. "I'll be back."

Gianna walked awkwardly to where her shoe lay on the ground and scooped it up. "What the fuck, Mayan." She yelled as the car started.

He cracked the window. "You thought your Principessa di Ghiaccio shit was funny. Well, payback is a hard cock smack to the chops. I pick the place tonight."

Standing there with her shoe in her hand, Gianna's chest rose and fell hard. Her voice cracked as she screamed, "Fuck you, Mayan. I wore this shit because I thought it would make you happy!" His chest cracked open as he watched her turn on her heel, grab her bag, and stomp toward the rooms.

Familiar anger filled the crack, and Mayan revved the engine loudly before peeling out of the motel parking lot. "She did it to make me happy?" He huffed loudly. "She's lying. She just didn't want to stay at that motel." He raked his hand through his dark hair, and his green eyes became sad, the patch in the crack breaking slightly with the possibilities. "I need a fucking drink and some titties," he said, picking up his phone to search for the nearest topless bar. "Anything to forget all of that mess."

After driving around for half an hour and asking a friendly gas station attendant with too much cologne, Mayan found himself in Wet Dreams. No search engine could tell you which club had the best tits and showed the most skin like a local could.

They aren't Chi-town girls… But they'll do. He thought as he watched the big watermelon-tittied redhead. Her face was well hidden behind her breasts as she hung upside down on the pole and slid down like a car with bad breaks. *It's a valiant attempt at a sloppy basic inverted.* He chuckled at the thought, his shoulders bobbing slightly. "I need to stop hanging out with strippers."

A low, throaty voice unexpectedly responded, "I agree." The soft tickle of her words on his ear made his cock swell, along with his rage.

Jerking his head away from her supple lips, he bit out, "Jealous? You couldn't even take your top off in front of a crowd." He paused, his lip curling with anger as he took in her infuriatingly gorgeous profile. Her head was still perched over his shoulder, and she was looking at the stage. Her hands rested on the back of his chair. Too close for comfort. "How did you find me?"

"Uber driver. Just had to ask for the best strip club in the area," she stated. She then pulled the back of the chair down, sending him plummeting to the sticky ground with a loud thud. His drink spilled across the small round table and onto the floor beside him, adding to the dirty, sticky mixture coating the floor.

Laying on the disgusting ground groaning, he watched her hips sway as she walked away.

"Fucking bitch," he hissed while staggering to his feet and picking up his chair.

His ass didn't even touch the seat before a topless waitress was bringing him a new drink with a questioning look. "Don't ask," he said through gritted teeth, accepting the napkins from her in one hand and the drink in the other. A small laugh escaped her pale pink lips before she smacked a hand over her mouth.

"I'm sorry. Don't be too embarrassed." She gave him a sympathetic smile. "We get plenty of angry wives coming in here and flying off the handle." Her smile broadened, and she gave him a quick wink. "Most aren't nearly as pretty as yours, though."

He choked on his drink, spurting a bit from his mouth. "No. No. You've got us wrong. She's nothing to me. Hardly even a friend."

She looked at him with her eyebrows raised and hand on her hip, "Mister. If anyone has what you two are wrong… It's you." Mayan looked into her sky-blue eyes, and his expression softened.

"No woman looks at a man the way she looks at you for nothing," she said with a tisk. With a swish of her long fire engine red hair, she turned and walked away, the bottom of her butt cheeks jiggling from the glittery royal blue cheekys.

Mayan shook his head in disbelief. "What kind of topless Yoda broads are you guys breeding in this state?" His deep green eyes scanned the room for G but found only the lights of the main stage changing to red. Captivated by the sinful color, he stopped searching for G and began watching.

Taking a deep drink of the whiskey, he leaned back, ready to forget Yoda and the bitch. A slight smirk curved his mouth when "I'm in Love with a Stripper, by T-Pain," started playing.

"Ah, the new girl anthem," he said, letting his sly tongue slowly caress his plump lips. *Maybe an out-of-town stress release is what I need,* he thought, sitting up in anticipation. His eyes widened in awe as the dark-haired temptress in high tops slowly swayed her hips to the music and approached the pole. She spun around it and sunk down into a squat with the bar at her back. There was only a tiny sheer black thong with a colorful butterfly on the front keeping every eye in the building from seeing the treasure beneath.

His gemstone eyes turned to soft green moss as hers locked onto his, and her heart-shaped lips pursed into a kiss, blown in his direction. He felt it smack into his face like a goddamn cartoon when she tucked her leg behind her and curled her body around the pole, spinning like a top until she stopped, her legs spreading into the splits, her taught ass cheeks slapping on the floor of the stage.

In the blink of an eye, she was up, and her matching bra was sliding down to her elbows. Her hands cupped her breasts innocently while she stared at the floor and sashayed to the pole to stand beside it.

Her eyes rose slowly, and a dangerous smile curved her lips. The bra fell, and her perfectly perky, rounded, mouthwatering breasts were killing him like a shot to the head.

His heart stopped, and his mind went to mush when, right before his eyes, she jumped up, grabbed onto the bar, and raised her feet above her head. Her thick legs slowly opened, spreading as wide as they could go. The entire room got a fantastic view of her heavenly mound, barely hidden behind the tiny sheer panties.

In his mind, a dirty rhyme played. *I would fuck her there, I would fuck her here, I would fuck her in the chair or destroy her in the air.*

The modest crowd went wild, and dollars rained across the stage; men whistled, and strippers cheered. Mayan watched as Gianna lowered herself from the pole, took a topless bow, grabbed her bra, and left the stage for the front door.

"Touché, you dumb bitch." Mayan adjusted himself while placing a hundred-dollar bill on the table and made for the parking lot to catch up with G. *I'll be taking her back to the motel,* he thought as he opened the door. The cold night wind greeted him while he watched a car turn out of the parking lot with G inside.

His teeth ground together, and his fists clenched. "Always running away."

He shook his head, got into his car, and then peeled out of the parking lot. Of course, he talked to himself on the way; it was already crazy. Talking to himself wouldn't hurt. "What the fuck was that?" His hand tightened on the steering wheel, and he took the turn a little too fast. His entire body was still buzzing with adrenaline from the show.

"She's so fuckin' stupid. Who does that?" He slammed his hand on the steering wheel. "Idiota! You don't know anyone out here.

Or what kind of crowd that place brings in. You could have been hurt!"

The light of the motel came into view, and his heart pounded harder against his chest. He was ready for this fight and prepared to tell her just how stupid she was for that little stunt.

The sound of gravel flying broke the silence of the night as Mayan skidded to a stop right in front of room number nine. He pushed open his door and jumped out, allowing it to bounce close behind him. His nostrils flared, and his chest rose and fell chaotically. Filled with fury, he thought, *this dumb bitch is going to learn her place. I won't try to save her again* before raising a foot to the door and stomping it open.

Wooden splinters flew as the door gave way, revealing Gianna. His heart pounded out of control, and the veins in his neck thickened like metal cords. She was standing there in her bra and panties. The same set she had just performed in. Her pretty black and Tiffany blue gun was raised and pointed right at him. *Fuck*. The gun, the girl, damn, the entire night, it was all too much.

"Mayan! What the fuck do you think you are doing breaking down my door?!"

She lowered the gun and brought her hands to her hips. "I could have shot you."

His muscles tensed, every hair on his body standing on end. The universe shifted around him; time slowed to a near-complete stop. He didn't care anymore.

The past had begun deteriorating the moment she got into his car. And now, seeing her standing there, her big, beautifully dark eyes staring into his, was a cocaine dust bath to his heart and dick.

In an instant, they beat the dog shit out of his brain. Destroying every bit of good sense he had. There was no way to bury it anymore. He was so absolutely in love with her that not having her had been feeding his hatred for her for all these years. With the past no longer standing in his way, he would have her, and anything or anyone that stood in his way would burn.

With a sudden rush of need, he forgot every word he was going to say to her and pounced after his prey. Clearing the distance between them in the blink of an eye, he slammed Gianna against the wall. Her soft body gave way under the press of his large muscular frame, and she gasped audibly, making his blood run hot, and his vision go nearly red. Palpable skin tingling, need consumed the hunter as the feminine noise registered.

He would have her; he would control her. Wrapping his hand around hers and the gun, he pinned it to the wall above her head while he pushed his groin into the heat of the apex of her thighs. Escape was now impossible. His mind was a blur; his body took over, raising his free hand to cup her face roughly while he pressed his lips to her gaping mouth. His tongue slid into her open mouth and over hers, demanding a response by reaching as far into her as he could. A smirk played on his lips as she complied, reaching just as far as he did. *That's a good girl.*

She bucked against him, and the friction against his thickening cock only encouraged his erection. *You're not getting away this time,* he thought savagely. Gianna's struggles continued to enhance his arousal. Primal instinct took over; *She is mine! And I will have what is mine!*

Pain spiked in his lower lip as her teeth bit into him. He ripped his mouth away, still panting with want. His head lolled down, and he pressed his face into the crook of her neck. Between pants, he huffed out, "That... was a very... bad girl, you bitchy little brat." He emphasized his point by nipping her neck hard enough to make her squeak. Releasing her skin, he said, "You'll pay for that."

He felt Gianna's chest rise against his own as she barked out a laugh.

"Aww, are you sick of playing with dirty strippers, Mayan?" Curving her back away from the wall, she attempted to buck him off. Her voice was strained as she pushed again. "I don't want you, Mayan, get the fuck off me."

He thrust forward, slamming her back into the wall. "Oh, you want it. I know you do." He lowered his voice to a rough growl and whispered while he rubbed his stubbled cheek against hers. "I think you're a dirty little slut."

Gianna growled and pushed her soft feminine curves against his hard, heated body, further exciting the predator within him. "Mmm, mhm, you're a dirty little slut, and you desperately want me to take what's mine. Take you and make you my good girl." He ran his open lips across her cheek and tapped his nose to hers.

"Don't you?"

"Fuck you, Mayan. If you let go of my hand, I'll show you just how much I don't want you," she said with a sneer.

Mayan's blood heated to a boil. He tilted his head and looked into her dark brown eyes. Then he softly brushed his lips against hers as he crooned, "I know how you like it, G. Do you want me to show you?"

Gianna let out a soft moan, and then, in a low, sultry voice, she purred,

"Ohh, Mayan. I'll show you just how bad I want you." Her hand suddenly jerked forward as she attempted to free her hand again. She growled and bared her teeth at him. "I want a bullet in you!"

Mayan placed his forehead on hers and tisked. "You want me to show you a better way to use that?"

Gianna rolled her eyes. "I can show YOU the best way."

Mayan smiled wide and pointed the gun down as he lowered their hands, sliding them between their bodies until they were snuggly between her thighs, the barrel pressing into her clit. His eyebrow quirked as he pushed it against her clit harder, his finger sliding with it. His cock hardened to its full extent, and his mouth began to water as he felt the wet fabric.

"Come on, G. If you behave, maybe I'll show you what good girls get," he said sweetly. She bit her lip and closed her eyes while Mayan continued to rub the barrel into her.

As he caressed her most sensitive spot with the cold steel, he felt his forearm graze against a patch of rough skin on her inner thigh. His mind raced to imagine everything that could have happened to leave such an ugly mark on a nearly unblemished masterpiece.

The small circular scar made him nearly feral, but he was drawn away by her response to his ministrations.

"Go fuck yourself, Mayan."

He let up a touch and then pushed the gun harder against her, making her hips jerk back, and a small cry escaped her parted lips.

Moving his mouth to her ear, he whispered. "I bet I can make you come right here. Right now. With only the gun." His tongue curled around her ear, and he felt her body shiver beneath him. "I did enjoy that little show you did for me… You liked being a naughty little skank, didn't you?"

Her body hesitantly sunk down, and she began moving her hips, rubbing herself on the gun and his knuckle. He could see it written on her face. She couldn't resist the forbidden temptation. Her body was demanding she give in to him. "Say it, G... say you're my good girl... say you're mine." He heard his own voice become almost pleading. "Say it, and I promise your cum will be leaking down the barrel."

Gianna moaned loudly and began sliding up and down the wall, desperately trying to gain release on her own. With a whimper, her lips caressed his ear, sending a shockwave of delight racing down to his groin.

"I've always been... your girl... since the day I met you."

Tingling overtook his entire body, and euphoria played on his nerves. Her words made his eyes roll to the back of his head. "That's right... you're my girl. And you want to be good for me, don't you?" Her tiny moans sped up, and he almost gave in to his temptation.

He wanted to push her down, spread her thick thighs apart, and force himself inside her.

To keep his self-control, he bit down on his lip and took a deep breath before saying, "You're going to be such a good girl, G, because you're going to come for me." His finger squeezed between her wet panties and the barrel, his large hand shielding her as he pulled the trigger and claimed her mouth with his.

Gianna's mouth fell open, her head tilting back as she screamed into his mouth in sheer ecstasy. Mayan looked at her in awe. The beauty in her climax stole his ability to breathe momentarily. The slick wetness of the precum that beaded on the head of his cock was torture. He imagined the sweet wet heat gathering on his head was the stream of cum that was running down the gun and slicking her thighs along with his hand.

Gianna panted heavily, her chest pressing against him as she caught her breath.

He slowly raised his hand to his mouth and slid two fingers into his mouth, sucking her cum off of them with a loud pop. "Fuck… you taste heavenly, G." Her eyes were wide with shock, but she bit her bottom lip.

She's loving every second of this. Pretend to be shocked and offended all you want, Principessa.
I know what a nasty little freak you really are, he thought with a smile before running his wet finger down her lips and crooning, "Next time… don't pull a gun on me, and I'll eat that pretty little pussy until you beg me to destroy you."

Gianna pressed her hands into his chest, pushing him back an inch. "There won't be a next time, Mayan."

His eyebrow rose at her declaration.

"Now get the fuck off me so I can grab my shit." He stepped back, granting her freedom from the wall. "Now that you shot the fucking gun, I'm sure the police are on their way, and I would prefer to be in fresh panties, dressed, and driving away before they get here." Her eyes nearly rolled out of her head as she shoved him back towards the door. "Giant oaf! Go take care of the manager."

Mayan raised his hands in surrender. "Alright, G, alright," he said, turning towards the door. Before he left, his eyes turned to slits, and he blew her a kiss. "If you make me go to another hotel instead of just sleeping a few hours at a truck stop, I will be coming for you again tonight." Gianna's lip curled in disgust. "We have some unfinished business," he said, adjusting himself and walking out the door to wait in the car.

Strutting confidently to the tiny management office, Mayan allowed the screen door to close loudly as he entered. Ashley dropped his cell phone while stuttering, "I... I... I'm sorry." while pushing the rolling chair back from the counter and away from the intimidating, muscled giant.

With a click of his tongue, Mayan waggled a finger at him before pointing to the phone and mouthing, "Finish the call, Ashley." Sweat began to fall down his greasy forehead. Lip twitching and eyes as big as saucers, Ashley nervously reached around his belly to the floor. Grabbing the phone, he brought it up to his ear.

"Sorry, sweaty hands, ya know. I'm nervous." Pausing for a moment while the other person spoke, he continued. "Yeah, gunshot; I'm not sure which room it came from."

His bug eyes never left Mayan's as he listened to the nine-one-one dispatcher.

Laughing to himself at the absurdity, Mayan made his way around the counter, slid behind the man who looked more like a giant shaking rolly-polly, and squatted down to rest his head on his shoulder.

Reaching into his pocket, Mayan felt the familiar cool sensation of his knife and caressed it with the pad of his thumb, like he had just done to Gianna.

Biting his lip in an attempt to get the unsatisfied beast under control, he listened as Ashley finished the call.

"Okay, I'll be in the office waiting. Thank you." Mayan slid the knife from his pocket with a soft, deadly click as the call ended.

With his head resting in the crook of Ashley's shoulder and neck, he could feel the man's blood racing through his carotid artery. His heart thudded against his chest, begging for Mayan to release it from its confines. *Not today,* he thought ruefully.

Bringing his arm up and around the man, he laid the razor-sharp steel against his dirty neck, just behind his ear. "I'm not going to kill you." Ashley's muscles loosened with that proclamation, further aggravating the already unsatisfied man on the edge of becoming feral.

Mayan angrily pressed the blade into the tender flesh, sliding it down just enough to leave an inch-long slice. Hot blood streamed down his neck, soaking into the cotton material of his dingy multi-stained tank top.

"I said I'm not going to kill you... and I won't." Stopping, Mayan took a deep breath and slowly exhaled, hoping it would take some of his frustration with it. It didn't.

"Listen here, you disgusting little pig," he said through gritted teeth, spittle spraying from his mouth. "I'm the big bad mother fucking wolf. And in this fairytale... the bad guy gets the girl."

Pulling his head away from the sniveling man, he spun the chair around. After two complete spins, he decided to stop its repetitive motion

He certainly didn't want the piece of shit throwing up on him. The palm of his hand made a loud thwap as it connected with Ashley's face. Squealing with terror, Ashley grabbed the offended cheek.

Blood pumped wildly through Mayan's veins, and he thrust his face inches from the tear-streaked face and snarled, baring his teeth.

Ashley jerked his head back and let out a terror-filled scream. "I won't tell… I promise!"

Mayans snarl turned to a feral smile, and he cooly stated, "You're goddamn right you won't."

Standing, he smoothed his hair back and pocketed his knife. "I JUST got the girl, little pig… you fuck this up for me-" Pausing, he poked the man's chest. "I'll come back, cut your heart from your chest, and make you watch me fuck it like a pocket pussy, while you die." Ashley's face turned from horror to astonished disgust right before his eyes.

Chuckling, Mayan smacked the man's cheek playfully, "I know, right?" With those words, he turned and headed for the door. Before exiting, he looked over his shoulder and added, "The most fucked up part about it, is that I mean it." His voice went low and cold. "I will happily come all over your blood-covered, spasming body if you take her from me."

The door slammed behind him, and Mayan walked with an undeniable pep in his step to the car, his girl already waiting inside. Cheerfully hopping in with a smile from ear to ear, he started it up and left his new favorite one-star motel.

"Manager taken care of?" She asked matter of factly.

With a sly wink, he replied, "Oh yeah. I don't think he would tell a priest during confession."

"I don't blame him. I want to forget, too."

"Liar! You loved every second of it." Gianna turned to stare out the window. She wouldn't be sucked into his game. Coaching himself through this weird interaction, he told himself, *she's still fighting, huh? Okay. She'll get over that soon enough—no need to push her.*

Seeing the uncomfortable confusion mar her sinfully gorgeous face, Mayan attempted to change the subject. "Want to know how I know he won't talk?"

Gianna bit her lip, clearly intrigued and wanting to hear the details. "I'm sure you charmed him, right? Some of that quick meathead wit?"

Laughing loudly, Mayan said, "Nope. I cut him. Then I told him I would rip his heart out and

fuck it if he did anything that took you from me."
As he spoke, he watched her eyes widen with
excitement, her hips squeeze together, and the
corner of her perfect bitch mouth curve up.
Waiting patiently for her to form words, the
thought *Oh, the things I'm going to make that
mouth do,* played on his mind.

When she was finally able to speak, he
listened while his bitchy brat lied her scrumptious
plump ass off. "None of that shit meant anything.
I'm not yours, and you're a special kind of fucked
up, get help," she said, curling her lip and
crossing her arms.

Having politely smiled through her
speech, Mayan cleared his throat loudly when she
was finished. "If you keep lying like that, I'm
going to put you over my knee." Gianna huffed
loudly, attempting to interrupt him.

His voice was booming and filled the car.
"Shut the fuck up, G!" Nostrils flaring with her
chest rising and falling fast, Gianna listened to
Mayan for once in her life. She shut her fucking
mouth.

Pushing his hair back, he continued. "You
are just as sick and twisted as I am. I bet you get
hot every time you pull that trigger." Gianna's
mouth fell open, but no words came out.

"We match G. Always have. Like it or not, no one will ever give you what I can.Now, am I stopping at a truck stop for some sleep? Or do you want to show me what a good girl you can be at a hotel?"

With a loud huff, she slumped into the seat. Squeezing her thighs together, she crossed her arms tight over her chest. Looking out the window, she replied in an adorably snotty tone. "You're wrong. I don't need anyone to match me. AND. I'll take the truck stop."

Mayan Gripped the steering wheel tighter and rolled his eyes.

I'm going to wear a hole in the leather protector before the end of this trip. Then he thought, *my girl loves the chase.* With a nod of his head, he cooed, "Have it your way, Principessa."

Chapter 6. Principessa

... This is awkward

Unsure of where they were or what time it was, Gianna brought one hand up to rub the sleep from her eyes and searched the side of the seat for the reclining buttons with the other. Finding it, she brought herself upright and groaned at the pain in her lower back. *I'm too old to be sleeping in cars, goddammit.*

"Good morning." Startled by the greeting coming from her window and not the driver's seat, Gianna instinctively placed her hand on her gun.

With a wide grin, Mayan shook his head. "Remember what happened last time you pulled a gun on me."

Rolling her eyes dramatically, Gianna groaned loudly. "Seriously, Mayan... stop, please. I don't want to go over this again."

Seeming to be wrestling internally, Mayan paused for a moment before saying, "Later, we can talk later. We have a lifetime."

Gianna's chest tightened, making it almost impossible to breathe.

How many years have I wanted to hear him tell me how much he wants me? How long have I wanted him to fight through my walls?

Deep inside, she felt the little bricklayer perk up, smack a hand against his work, and say, these walls won't be coming down. Especially not for him. The door opened and closed, startling her from her thoughts. She looked over and found him staring at her legs.

"What?" She asked, scooping up her phone and opening her favorite mind-numbing, adorable game to distract herself.

Watching him from the corner of her eye, she unconsciously started biting her lip at the sight of his jaw working. Seeing him growing agitated never failed to bring her knees together. *I am fucked up,* she thought with a grin.

An hour of silence had gone by when suddenly Mayan cleared his throat loudly. "I'm sure they are dead now, but who shot you in your thigh?" A growl of frustration escaped him, and his body became rigid. "If they aren't dead, they will be soon."

The question was unexpected, but the promise of death in his eyes was why it had always been impossible to let him go. Torn between wanting to straddle him and wanting to choke him for his hand in her pain, Gianna stayed silent.

Apparently, for too long. "If you don't tell me, I'll find out on my own," he said in a dark, whispered threat.

Her anger spiked with his words, making her choice an easy one. "It's none of your fucking business," she said, putting her phone down, crossing her arms, and turning to the window.

Mayan laughed haughtily, "Perhaps you have forgotten this about me…" Like a light, Mayan switched from laughing to screaming, the veins in his neck protruding. "I get what I want!"

You want it? You got it fuck boy!

Heart pounding hard enough to make her body shake with anger, Gianna yelled, "You want to know?" Throwing her arms out, she began to let it all out. "It might as well have been you!" Mayan's face pinched in confusion. "After you saved the day, my father said I needed to learn that no one can save me."

Seeing the pain bloom on his face enraged her further. Her nails dug deep into her palms. "It's your fault. After that, I was never truly my father's Principessa again. We will always have that between us." Her eyes began to tear, but none fell. They never would again. "You took my dad from me and made it impossible for me to ever love you."

Her chest fell, and her shoulders slumped. Sitting back into the seat, she stared out the windshield, refusing to acknowledge the anguish her confession had brought him. "I can never forgive you."

With growling stomachs and heavy hearts, Mayan and Gianna pulled into the Golden Nugget parking garage. Shoving the door open, Gianna stepped out of the Lotus, taking the full heat of Vegas in the summer to the face." Oh, oh, that's disgusting. People live here?" She said, wiping the beads of sweat that quickly formed on her brow away and pulling her thick hair up off her neck. Mayan laughed while pulling her luggage from the car with his duffle bag.

"Oh, come on, G. Just put those itty-bitty shorts back on, and you'll be fine." He ended with a raised eyebrow while biting his plump lower lip.

Blood racing to everywhere except her brain, Gianna stumbled forward but managed to sputter out, "I... uhh... wouldn't wanna... you know... cut off what little blood supply your brain gets." She could feel his eyes on her as she continued to the lobby door, almost as though his hands were caressing her hips and matching her effortlessly seductive sway with each step.

Looking up, Gianna could only imagine how beautiful the front entrance lights would be at night. The front door opened, and three large Q-tip-headed old bitties came spilling out while cackling. "I'm going to get me one of them lap dances, Ethel. I'm not backing down this time." One declared.

"You ain't getting no lap dance, Lucy. You'll have a damn heart attack if you try." A woman with a gold fanny pack replied, making the other two burst out in howling laughter.

Gianna stood to the side while she watched Mayan.

"Hello," he said, dipping his chin at them. A sly snake smile spread on his face, making the white heads come to a squeaking halt. "How lucky of me to run into three gorgeous ladies on my first day here."

"Hot diggity daffodil boy. You're a big boy, aren't ya?" Said the one Gianna had to assume was Lucy.

"Yes, ma'am. My mama fed me well, I guess," he said with a shrug.

The woman with the gold fanny pack fanned herself with her hand. "Listen here, boy," she began, looking Mayan up and down appreciatively. "You're a doll. That's for certain. But. You're going to have to get out of our way unless you're going to start stripping or spilling coins out your drawers."

Gianna watched Mayan's eyebrow raise. "With all due respect, ladies. If I start taking my clothes off, you'll be the ones dropping coins from your panties." As the ladies erupted into laughter, Gianna snuck by into the lobby. *I'll just wait here.* She thought while her eyes rolled. *Leave it to Mayan to rile up some little old ladies while we have a job to do.*

No more than a minute later, Mayan came through the doors with a smile from ear to ear. "I can't help it. I love messing with rowdy seniors."

She couldn't help but smile. He had his good side. His soft spots. "I'm sure you do. Be careful, Mayan. You might end up with an overzealous GILF one day."

Mayan's face curled as he walked up to the front desk. "Not my type G. So don't get jealous." Before she could respond, Mayan began speaking to the twenty-something pink-haired woman behind the desk.

"Hello, welcome to the golden nugget. Do you have a reservation with us?"

"I do. It's under Mayan Russo."

Typing into the computer as he spoke, she smiled brightly. "Alright, I have you right here. Executive room with a king-size bed. Correct."

Gianna's mouth dropped open to protest the single room, but Mayan turned to her, a stern look on his face, brooking no room for argument. His voice lowered. "We are supposed to be 'Together'. I'll sleep on the floor if I have to. Just shut up and go with it."

Turning back to the puzzled lady, Mayan smiled. "Sorry about that. Yes, king-size bed."

"Umm, okay. Room three hundred and ten. Here are your entry keys," she handed him two cards.

"Great, can I get someone to bring our bags up? We have a lunch date we have to get to."

"Absolutely. I'll take those and have someone bring them to your room." She said, grabbing the bags from Mayan.

"Thanks so much." Putting his hand on the small of her back, Mayan handed her a key card and ushered Gianna through the lobby.

"Listen. If I have to sleep on the floor, I will. But we need one room because we are supposed to be on a getaway together."

Seriously aggravated, Gianna asked, "Where are we going? What lunch?"

Mayan replied while opening the door for her. "Roman and Lyla. We are having lunch with them, and he will give us the information we need."

If she wasn't sweaty enough before, she certainly was now walking into the sunny pool area. Mayan gave a short wave and squeezed her hip, earning a jab to the ribs. "Alright, that was fair." He said through gritted teeth.

Smiling, Gianna spotted the big, dark-haired brute that matched Mayan across the way, seated at a small table with a giggling brunette. *That must be Lyla,* she thought with a shake of her head. *He would pick a chipper chit to fall for*.

As they approached the table, Mayan extended a hand to Lyla. "Hi, you must be Lyla," he said with a firm shake of her hand, then gestured to Gianna. "This is G. She's known my brother and me since we were kids."

Lyla smiled at Gianna, then looked between her and Mayan. "It's nice to meet you both. Roman has told me so much about you." She seemed to become uneasy, her feet shifting and eyes darting anywhere but Gianna and Mayan. "Sorry, we uhh... had to meet like... this."

Roman laughed loudly. "Sorry, Lye, we just aren't the Sunday dinner kind of crowd." Seeing Lyla playfully smack Roman's arm and the sparkle that came to his eyes made Gianna's cold heart warm. *I'm glad he found someone. Someone who is as sweet as him. He never belonged with us.* Her smile dropped at the thought. *Us? Mayan and I are not an us. We never were.*

Standing between Lyla and Mayan, Roman patted his brother's shoulder, then began to fidget awkwardly with a lock of Lyla's hair. "Why don't we take a walk, Mayan? We have a lot to talk about."

Lyla's eyes shot to Roman's. "Now isn't the time. Why don't you wait until all the nasty business is done?" Roman gave a curt nod, then looked between Gianna and Mayan.

"She's right. We will have plenty of time to talk after." Mayan shrugged his shoulders and looked at Roman.

Roman's face suddenly scrunched into a scowl, and he laughed as though he was taking a good look at them for the first time. "Wow. You guys really didn't dress for the pool lunch, did you?" He shook his head. "This isn't all work. Come on, Mayan, let's go buy you and G a suit."

Looking down at her pretty pink heels and black skinny jeans, she wondered to herself. *What the fuck? He isn't even a little curious about what Roman wanted to talk about?* Gianna's eyes widened. *Is she pregnant?*

When she finished inspecting her clothes and her speculative pondering, she looked up and saw Mayan walking away with Roman. Panicked, she called after them, "You mean I have to stay here with her?" she said, with a jerk of her head towards Lyla. They didn't even acknowledge her; they just kept walking like they couldn't hear her. "Pricks!" she yelled, then turned to find Lyla scowling, holding two red slushie drinks.

"Well. Now I have to drink two drinks since you want to be a bitch," Lyla said as she sat and slurped loudly, ending with a big "Ahhh." Gianna's eyebrow shot up, and she could feel the rumble of laughter start in her chest. *I guess she's not pregnant.*

"Wow, I'm guessing Roman didn't tell you much about us since you're brave enough to talk to me like that."

She sat across from Lyla and crossed her arms with a tilt of her head, enjoying the challenge that the sweet pea was offering.

Smiling sweetly Lyla pushed the other drink to Gianna. "Oh, he told me, I just don't give a shit. What are you going to do? Shoot me at the pool?" She questioned with a doofy look while rolling her eyes.

Gianna brought the drink to her lips and savored every drop of the frozen strawberry margarita and the cooling sensation it brought to her overheated body. Lowering the cup, she stared directly into Lyla's soft brown eyes. "No, nothing like that. I would find your room and then strangle you with my bare hands. That way, I'm the last thing you ever see, and I get to watch the light leave your eyes."

Satisfied with Lyla's jaw hitting the floor, Gianna took another quick sip and then attempted to calm the situation down. "I'm playing, Lyla. Sorry, I was rude. I had a long, awkward drive here." Lifting her glass in a toast, she ended with, "I am happy to see Roman found a sweet girl with a mouth on her, though."

Lyla visibly relaxed and took two large gulps of her drink. "Oh, thank God, with everything I've heard about you and Mayan, I wasn't sure how serious you were."

"I'm sure everything you've heard is true," Gianna stated with a sly grin. "What's with the pool meeting?" she asked, looking around at all the tourists and families. "Afraid I would kill you if we weren't in a public setting?"

"No. I wanted to sit by the pool if I had to do this." Lyla paused and chewed on her lower lip. "I mean. That was before he told me about Mayan's scar." Lyla looked almost pleading, extending a hand across the table to Gianna. Gianna moved back instinctively. "I mean. I can see why it was an awkward ride for the two of you."

Thoroughly confused, she asked, "What does Mayan's scar have to do with us being awkward? And didn't Roman tell you that Mayan isn't insecure about it?" She rolled her eyes, "It's kind of his calling card." She watched as Lyla's face scrunched up, and she became uneasy. *What is wrong with this broad?*

Lyla's jaw dropped for a second time, forming a perfect O. Bringing one hand to her mouth and the other to her chest, she whispered, "I don't think I should say."

Gianna's jaw tightened, her teeth clenching together almost painfully. "If you don't, I'll have to do more than just threaten you, Lyla. I'm getting very annoyed with this very fast."

Grabbing at her hair, Lyla stared down at the table. "Fuck. Fuck. Fuck." She looked up and reached across the table again. This time, catching Gianna's hand before she could move back. Staring directly into her eyes, Lyla began, "Okay, but please don't tell Roman I fucked up. I didn't know *you* didn't know."

Looking into her eyes, Gianna couldn't help but feel safe, like Lyla was secretly whispering that she wasn't trying to hurt her. And that made her extremely uncomfortable. *No one is this nice.* "Mayan's scar…" She paused with an audible gulp. "Your father did that to him after he saved you." Words were coming from Lyla's mouth, but Gianna wasn't sure she was hearing them correctly. "He told him that his heart would get him in trouble and he needed a reminder that would stay forever." Lyla shook her head with a loud exhale. "No offense. But your dad's fucked."

Gianna pulled her hand from Lyla and stood abruptly. *Called it. Too good to be true.* "Tell them I needed a nap," she stated firmly, then walked rigidly to the lobby.

The world around her smeared, nothing stayed in focus as she walked. She was surprised when she found herself in an elevator with squawking people on either side of her. She had no idea what those people were saying. It was as though words had no meaning.

Her mind was too busy trying to comprehend what she had just learned. *How could he... he... I... How do I come back from this?* The doors opened, and her feet stumbled beneath her as she exited. Her subconscious mind began instructing her body. *Three ten, three ten, get to room three ten, three ten. Don't stop.*

Gold numbers on flying doors hardly registered, but her mind had just enough power and sanity left to grab them and hold on— *Three oh eight, Three oh nine.*

Pressing her forehead to the door marked three ten that stood between her and the bed, Gianna pulled the card key from her pocket and placed it in front of the card reader. The handle became slick with the sweat of her palm as she pushed it down, revealing her freedom from prying eyes.

Gianna ran to the bed, wrapping herself around a pillow and smashing her face into another. But it was no use; tears, real tears, the ones she had sworn never to let free, fell. Inaudible sounds spilled from her as she sobbed, her hatred for Mayan ripping her apart and growing into shame. "He hurt us both." She sobbed.

Gianna bit down on her lip to keep the awful words from springing to life as they jumped from her lips. But there was no stopping it.

The truth had finally surfaced, and there was no hiding from it. "Mayan didn't take you from me... You did!" She yelled, her body shaking with grief, rage, and embarrassment.

Gentle fingertips glided across her clammy forehead startling Gianna awake. With her heart pumping and mind spiraling, her rigid body jerked back from the intrusive touch.

"I'm sorry. I didn't mean to startle you." Gianna stared at Lyla without words, her eyes as wide as they could go. "I didn't want Mayan to come up here and check on you," Lyla said softly. "I figured you needed time to digest the shit bomb I just dropped on you."

She couldn't keep her chest from visibly rising and falling, infuriating her. *You're a goddamn killer. Get yourself under control!* Lyla forced a small smile. "I know that look." Her eyes went to the bed.

"I know you don't know me. But I've been through a lot lately." Lyla's eyes rose and locked with Gianna's. Gianna's heart slowed, and her breathing steadied. "I've been in the 'what the fuck just happened to my life' spiral."

She laughed softly and raised a finger, beginning to count. "One, my husband disappeared." She raised another finger. "Two, his assistant was stealing money from me." Raising the last finger, her eyes rolled, and she swayed her head from side to side. "Well, anyways, long story short, he was fucking the assistant, and she tried to have him killed, then tried to kill me and finish him off." Her shoulders shrugged, and she sighed loudly. "So, she shot him in front of me, and I held him while he died."

Gianna swore softly, "Fuck." and her muscles loosened. "Your life is shit."

Lyla's eyebrows bunched together. "Well. I know. But, like, you don't have to be a cunt."

With a sharp intake of breath through gritted teeth, Gianna winced. She curled around the other again. "I don't mean to be a cunt, Lyla. But I don't people." She closed her eyes in an effort to run from the reality she now lived in. A soft hand lay on hers, pulling her mind back to the uncomfortable present. Tiny hairs on her arm raised at the contact, and she pulled her hand back, her eyes popping open.

Her lip curled, "You're a toucher, huh?"

"WOW." Lyla pushed a hand through her hair. "I'm guessing you don't have friends."

"I don't need friends." Her eyes turned to slits, and her chin raised. "I'm not that weak."

A loud belly laugh erupted from Lyla, her shoulders bobbing as she grabbed her stomach. "I think you don't have friends because you *are* weak." Gianna's nostrils flared, and her blood heated to a boil as she watched Lyla shrug with a nonchalant look. "Loving people is hard, and you have to be vulnerable."

Gianna was pissed, but she gained a small amount of respect and admiration for the woman in front of her. *Maybe she's right. Maybe I am weak; I did let my father take Mayan from me. I let him take them all from me.*

"Listen, G, can I call you G?" She asked. Gianna nodded her head absent-mindedly, still stuck in her own world. "Listen, G, you found out some fucked up shit. And it seems like you don't have anyone to talk to about it." Lyla grabbed her hand forcefully. Gianna's body tensed at the physical connection.

"I'm here. I don't know if you know how important you are to Roman." She shook Gianna's hand, forcing her to look her in the eyes. "He loves you. And if you're important to him, you're important to me."

I'm important to Roman? Still? After everything? The thought made Gianna's broken heart pound painfully. "Gianna!" Blinking her eyes rapidly, she realized she had begun to stare off into space.

"I don't know what to do, Lyla." She gently took her hand back. "I don't do this." She said, waving a hand between them.

"It's super apparent."

Gianna chuckled, but pain filled her dark eyes. "What do I do? Why didn't he tell me?"

Smiling, Lyla responded, "I'm sure he didn't want you to have to bear that burden. Imagine if you knew then what you know now."

Thinking back, she remembered her hatred for her father, quickly transferring to Mayan. Mad at him for trying to save her, mad at him for forcing her father's hand. *I was an idiot. It was never Mayan.* "He would have taken away what little bit of your father you had left."

A tear rolled down her cheek. "He gave me my father and let me hate him."

Looking thoughtful, Lyla put a finger on her chin. "I suspect he hated you too." She traced an imaginary X on her chest with her finger. "The whole 'X' on his chest for loving you thing, probably took a while to get over."

"I'm sure I gave him more reasons to hate me after that." She took a deep breath and let out an audible sigh. "So, what now?" Her eyes searched Lyla's face for an answer. "What do I do about him?" She paused and dropped her head into her hands. "What do I do about my fucking father?"

"Oh, I have no idea. I hardly had a father. I definitely didn't have a mob boss to deal with." Both their heads shot to the door at a loud knock.

"Hey, everything okay?" Roman said through the door.

"Yeah, I'll be right there." Lyla stood and turned towards the door but stopped and looked over her shoulder. "As for Mayan... I would let him love you." She turned, and as she went to the door, she said, "You guys are two fucked up peas in a weird ass pod." Flinging the door open, Lyla stepped out and pushed Roman back into the hall. "It's all good, honey. Just some girl talk."

Gianna's heart leaped as Mayan stepped in, grabbing the key card from Lyla as he entered. *Oh fuck. Fuck. Don't say shit. Please, dear lord, I hope he doesn't say anything.*

Walking to the light oak table next to the matching dresser, Mayan grabbed his duffle bag and headed for the bathroom.

"You feeling okay? Lyla said you got all white and said you had to nap. She thought it might be… umm… something about woman troubles, so she came up here to check if you needed anything."

"Oh, yeah, I'm fine." She said, scooting off the bed and going to her luggage. *I hope he doesn't smell me. I certainly can smell myself,* she thought, with a wrinkle of her nose.

"Okay, cool. So, are you up for finishing the job?"

Gianna spun around and found Mayan's smiling head sticking out of the bathroom. "That's right. I got the information already."

"I can't wait to see that little shit," Gianna said with a growl.

"Good. We can shower and then go." Mayan winked. "Come on, princess, let me wash you." His eyes traveled her body from head to toe, "Or better yet. Why don't you wash your prince and then get on your knees like a good girl."

Holy fuck. Yes, sir, went through her mind as she nibbled on her bottom lip. But "There isn't enough bleach in this hotel to clean you" is what came out of her mouth when it opened.

Mayan shrugged and closed the door, saying, "I'll get ya. I got time."

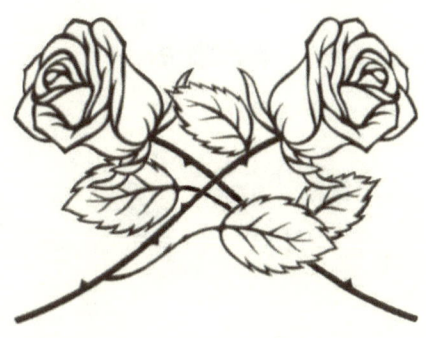

< Messages **Seppie** Details

Hey, girl. Tio wants to know what's up.

If he wants to know, he can ask.

He's not up to it. He's been under the weather. More so than usual.

Do I need to leave? Or do you have it under control?

96% ▇▇

‹ Messages **Seppie** Details

Naw. I got this. I just need to know what you're up to.

I have arranged a messy dinner date for tonight. But I'll be home soon

She threw her phone on the side table and started getting ready for the night. They wouldn't be bringing their phones. If they brought them, their movements would be easily accessible.

One would think that a man on the run would know better than to walk the streets at night all alone... I guess he isn't that smart after all.

Gianna stealthily glided up beside him, matching his strides. Startled by the familiar soft hand caressing his forearm, Stefan dropped his phone and grocery bag to the ground. If he wasn't so cheap and had just ordered in, he wouldn't have been such an easy target. Pressing the cold, hard barrel of her gun into his soft side, Gianna grabbed Stefan's forearm and tugged him close.

"Did you miss me, baby?" Her lips pursed into a dramatic pout, and her eyes widened like a sad puppy dogs.
"Or did you find someone new in the FBI?" Deviant pleasure rippled through her as Stefan began to tremble.

Her eyes flashed with mischief and locked on Mayan as her tongue darted out and curled around the shell of his ear. She watched as he approached them and wrapped his arm around Stefan's shoulder. Shooing Gianna back with his hand, Mayan smacked Stefan's ear with a loud thwap, making him whimper loudly. Licking at her lips, Gianna looked past Stefan.

"Aww. You don't like it when I touch other boys?"

"You know I don't. But you love making me see red. Don't you?"

Stefan's watery blue eyes turned to Giann. His voice was small and pathetic as he said, "I'm sorry. I'm so sorry. They haven't even done any of the process." His head swung between them. "I swear. They said they had to verify my involvement before they would consider me." His voice cracked with a burst of emotion. "I won't do it. I swear. Please, Gianna. Please don't…" Stefan's pleas for his life trailed off as the lights of the suburban food market glinted off Mayan's knife.

"Don't fuckin interrupt me while I'm talking to my girl, you little shit."

"Your girl?" Both Stefan and Gianna questioned in unison.

Mayan turned the shaking man toward a small blue Prius, "Come on, Stefan. You're not a suburban boy. Let's get you back to the city. Where you belong."

"Sh- sh- Chicago?" Mayan sent Stefan flying into the car's passenger side with a tiny nudge.

"Open it up and get in. G, take him to the hotel. I'm not driving that pile of crap." Mayan wrapped an arm around Gianna's waist and pulled her close, crushing his hard muscles against her plush curves.

Soft, plump lips brushed against her cheek, sending a wildfire sensation dancing through her entire body.

She watched his hand raise to her face and push a stray strand away before he grabbed her chin between his thumb and pointer, tilting it upward. Trying to disobey his unspoken command, she looked to the side.

"Look at me," he said sternly. Reluctantly obeying him, she stared straight into his sparkling green eyes. They scanned hers, and she could feel him searching inside her. "You took my soul years ago, Principessa, and I've never wanted it back. It belongs with you."

His words smashed the long-standing barriers like a bomb in a shoe box. Before the tiny, angry brick mason could begin to repair the walls, her body pushed harder into Mayan, forcing him to take a step back.

Wrapping herself around his broad body and sinking her lips onto his, her tongue explored the depths of his mouth passionately. Her lips pressed harder onto his, reaching as far back as she could. There wasn't one inch of him she would leave untouched. Her hands grasped at his thick, black hair and pulled, forcing him to open wider.

As she wrapped a leg around his, Mayan's hand pressed against her hip, pushing her back and breaking the kiss abruptly. Panting heavily, he stepped away from her. "Soon. But not yet."

Gianna frowned and crossed her arms over her chest. "That's cute that you think you tell me what happens between us, and when it happens."

Mayan shot her a stony glare. "Because I do tell you. You'll learn that sooner or later."

Turning away with a huff of defiance, she purposely swayed her hips more and slid her hands along her curves to her plump ass, placing her hands innocently into her back pockets. *If you're going to tell me to wait, I'm going to make every second torture.*

With that thought, she looked over her shoulder with a smirk. "See you there, limp dick."

Jumping into the driver's seat, she closed the door and blew a small air kiss at Stefan as she started the car. "Time for a field trip to Freemont Street, baby."

After a lengthy car ride with Gianna telling the graphic story of how she got the bag of hands in the first place, Stefan seemed ready to welcome death. Satisfied with the ghost-white look of disgust on his face, Gianna pulled up under the conveniently broken streetlight and shut off the car.

Looking around the darkened street, she wondered aloud, "Hmm… don't tell me this shitty Prius beat the lovely lady lotus."

From the shadows just beyond the crumbling sidewalk and on the other side of the chain-link fence enclosing one of the many abandoned hotels on East Fremont Street, a sinfully yummy dark voice slithered down her spine. "I wouldn't take her here; unlike you, she's a lady."

Pushing the car door open with her foot, Gianna giggled. "That's not bad. Did it take you the entire car ride to think of it?"

Walking around the car with a little more sway in her hips than usual, Gianna trailed a finger on the hood and looked back at the darkness over her shoulder. With a swipe of her tongue over her lips, she cooed, "No lady would have you."

Reaching the passenger door, her hand gripped the warm handle of the gun in her waistband while she yanked Stefan forcibly from the car and pressed it into his kidney. The sheer joy his sniveling brought to her should have made her worry. But she would need a conscience for that. Instead, there was only a tiny cheerleader hopping up and down, screaming to gut him like the yellow-bellied fish he was.

Gianna crossed the street to the fence with the shaking man stumbling before her, casually glancing around to ensure their anonymity.

Pushing Stefan through the gap in the fencing, Gianna smiled up at the dark man towering over them from just beyond the fence. "You're not the smartest, but you are pretty. I'll give you that."

Mayan grabbed Stefan's shirt and pulled him through the gap, making him cry out in pain as the wires tore through the soft fabric. "And so what if it did take me the entire time? I'm pretty proud of it."

Slinking through the gap in the fence like a stealthy cat, she giggled into her hand. "Oh wow, well, that really got under your skin, huh?"

As she stood, Stefan looked between them. With his eyebrows in his hairline and his eyes as big as dinner plates, Stefan yelled, "What the hell even is going on?"

His shirt ripped with a loud tearing sound, leaving a piece of frayed fabric in Mayan's clenched fist as he bolted away from the pair.

Screaming in her head, *Oh hell no!* Gianna took off after him, launching herself onto his back and sending him skidding on his face across the deeply pitted asphalt.

Sitting atop his back, she slid her hand into his sweaty hair and pulled his head back to see his bloodied face as she brought her lips to his ear. "Where you going, baby? The fun hasn't even started yet."

Footsteps sounded from behind her, and she heard Mayan growl, "I cannot begin to tell you how much hearing you call another man baby makes me want to cut him into tiny pieces the size of cheese cubes."

The excitement rushing throughout her body only heightened as she felt Mayan kick Stefan between his legs.

Between hearing Mayan's words, Stefan's pathetic cries, and the feeling of thrusting forward while straddling him, she could feel herself clench as she dampened her panties.

If he doesn't like me calling him baby… I wonder what he would do if I ground my pussy against his back.

"G, come on, get off him so we can get him inside," Mayan said, pulling her from her naughty thoughts while he put one foot on Stefan's back and a hand under her arm to help her up.

Just that simple touch from him made her skin tingle. *Fuck. I've gone insane,* she thought, but then quickly amended it. *I've always been fucked up.*

But he… he makes me absolutely mad in a way I've never known. I wonder if he'll run when he sees just how fucked I've become. As she stood, Mayan bent down to grab the bloodied man and usher him into the abandoned nineteen seventies motel.

Walking behind the men into the lightless structure, she placed her hands on Mayan's waist while her eyes adjusted. Feeling the deep indents at the top of his pants with her fingertips made her want to explore further. Mayan groaned slightly as she brought herself closer to him, pushing her chest into his back.

"I can give you money," Stefan whined.

Mayan laughed. "Fuck your money. You know the rules of the life, kid."

Feeling the deep laugh rumble through him at the crying man fanned the always present hidden dark flame within her. Biting her lip, she attempted to slide one hand down between his thighs.

Unfortunately, right as her hand began its descent, he opened the door to the room they had set up, spilling bright light into the hallway and momentarily blinding her. Bringing her hands up to shield her eyes, she groaned loudly as the men walked further into the room.

"God damn, I'm pretty sure my eyeballs just disintegrated. How many lanterns did you put in here?"

Pushing Stefan down into the chair positioned in the middle of the room, Mayan shook his head. "You really are a princess, aren't you? There are only two. Your eyes are fine."

Bringing her hands down to her hips, Gianna walked into the empty room and stood before the men, watching as Mayan strapped her mistake into the chair. Staring at the disgusting little worm she had been stupid enough to allow into her life, she began to see her father.

Stefan's slim face and pointed chin suddenly became rounded. She actually heard his thick accent while his double chin wiggled.

"You should have known better. Just one more way you've disappointed me." Gianna's breath quickened, and her heart began to pound. She was sixteen again, and her father stood strong and intimidating above her. She was on the ground clutching her leg as hot blood gushed from her thigh. Tears blurred her vision as the sting of betrayal truly sunk in.

No gunshot could be more painful than the shame ripping through her chest as her hero told her, "You're weak, Principessa."

No longer able to hold her head up, she laid her face against the cool grass, soothing her reddened cheek. "You did this. It wasn't supposed to be like this."

Attempting to look up, she could hardly make him out as he knelt in the pooling blood beside her. "You needed to learn how much pain life will bring. And better yet, that no one can stop it." The heat of his breath hit her face, telling her that he had brought his face to hers. But her eyelids were too heavy to move. "Not even that little shit Mayan can spare you the pain life brings. Save yourself next time. If not, then you're not worth the life I gave you, and I'll take it."

Hearing him talk about Mayan that way had bit at her heart back then. But now, as a grown woman, it infuriated her.

I was a child... he was a child! We were in love, and your anger and pride took that from us! Body shaking with rage, Gianna gripped the gun in her waistband and stepped forward and back into the warped reality where her father was strapped into the chair before her.

"Move Mayan." He must have seen the promise of death on her face because Mayan didn't speak; he moved, walking to stand behind her.

Bringing the tip of the gun to his thigh, Gianna leaned in, her lips only an inch from his ear.

Tightening her grip, she slowly squeezed the trigger. "No one can save you, Papa."

Hot blood sprayed her hand and ran down to the floor as Stefan's wounded face twisted with pain, "What the fuck?! You crazy bitch. You've fuckin lost it! I'm not your fucking dad."

Mayan moved swiftly around Gianna while bringing his knife out. "She's having a moment, but no one talks to my girl that way." Gianna watched as he grabbed Stefan's shirt, tore a piece, and squatted down in front of him. With a wink, Mayan whispered, "She's crazy as hell, but I'm worse. Say 'ahh'."

There was nowhere for him to go, and there was nothing he could do to stop him.

Frantic screaming spilled from Stefan as Mayan shoved the cloth into his mouth, wrapped it around the tip of his tongue, and pulled it out past his quivering lips. Looking over his shoulder at her, he said, "See, you gotta get a cloth to hold the tongue. Otherwise, the slimy little sucker will slip right out of your hand." His voice was like dark velvet, caressing every depraved part of her black soul. "Tell me, G. Tell me you want me to."

Desperate to ground herself during the high of insanity, Gianna slid her gun back into her waistband and ran her hands back and forth on Mayan's tight shoulders. "Do it, Mayan. I want you to do it so Papa can never hurt us with his words."

The chair began to rattle and pound on the floor as his victim suffered through the unfiltered pain. Stephans screams became gurgles as blood filled his mouth. The sound of thick muscle separating as Mayan sawed and pulled at his tongue could barely be heard. Feeling the vibration, hearing the drowning screams, and watching the tears spill down Stefan's face as Mayan slid his switchblade back and forth across his tongue took away the illusion of her father.

She always knew her heart was his, buried and hidden away, but she never knew how much she could love. Until he took the chunk of muscle and shoved it and the cloth into the mouth of the worm, they had come all this way for.

Mayan patted Stefan's cheek. "I think that cloth in there should help with the bleeding a little." He shrugged. "Or not. I don't actually know, but we're going to find out."

Placing her hands on either side of his face, she tilted Mayan's head to the side.

She stared down at the blood-speckled face of the man she had told herself she despised above all others for a moment. "God damn, you're disgusting and disturbed... I love it." She said softly before licking the side of his face clean with a broad stroke of her tongue.

Reaching his hand above his head, he pushed it into her hair and cradled her head while he looked up at her from the corner of his eye. "I fuckin' knew you loved me, you bratty bitch."

Gianna attempted to push herself away from him, only to find his hand fisting her hair firmly. Glaring at him defiantly, she blankly stated, "I said IT. Not. YOU."

Without warning, Mayan's other arm came up between her legs as he pulled her down to the ground in front of him. Slightly dizzy, Gianna quickly realized she was laid out on the ground.

Neatly presented to the demon kneeling above her. The look in his eyes was wild with hunger.

Staring into his eyes, Gianna accepted the unspoken challenge. *I'll feed you. I'll give you precisely what you've been missing.* "Ohh, look at you. Big bad man threw the helpless princess to the ground. Does that make you feel big?" While propping herself up on an elbow, she allowed her eyes to travel down to his crotch. "Does it make your little dick hard?"

With a deep growl, Mayan jumped on top of Gianna, his knees pressing hard into her shoulders as he pinned her down. A scream of pain and shock tore from her throat. Squirming beneath him as she attempted to free herself, Gianna felt the stinging of splinters stabbing into her skin from the old, unkept wood floors. Unwilling to submit without a fight, she brought her knee up and into his back as hard as she could.

With a disgustingly satisfied smirk, Mayan smiled down at her, then smacked her cheek just hard enough to make the skin sting, and her struggle stopped in utter surprise. |

"Don't say a fuckin word, G."

Gianna's heart thumped against her chest. The thrill of being trapped beneath him and being forced to comply, was one she had never known she needed. Biting her bottom lip, she waited for him to speak.

The only sound in the room was the sobbing and struggling of the rat behind her. Gianna's eyes widened as Mayan's hand came down again, her eyes instinctively closing tight in anticipation of the reprimand.

The delicious heat of the slap never came, though. Instead, she felt the cool, scarred skin of his knuckles slide across her cheek, soothing the burning skin.

"That's my good girl. I'm going to show you, AND that sniveling prick, what it is you need."

Lava traveled through her veins with his words. The need to defy and irritate him outweighed the longing to obey long enough to feel what he thought she needed. "And you think you know what I need?" She let out a short laugh. "Doubtful."

Squirming in a half-hearted attempt to escape, she tilted her head back to see Stefan as she put the cherry on the Sunday. *Ooo, baby, get ready to see red.* "How about I put my pretty wet pussy on the sniveling prick's delicious cock and give you some pointers?"

Looking at Stefan for a second longer, her smile went from ear to ear, feeling Mayan's knees dig harder into her. Ready to see the smoke pouring from his ears, Gianna moved her chin down to her chest, bringing her face to face with Mayan's bejeweled, precum-dripping cock.

Oh fuck...

She didn't have time for any other thought. His knees were just beneath her armpits in the blink of an eye. His hand clamped around her throat, forcing her to gasp for air, giving him a literal opening to ram his dick down her throat.

She didn't feel the pools of tears in her ears from her watering eyes, didn't feel the bite of yet another splinter wiggling its way beneath her skin. What she did feel was the throbbing veiny cock, fucking her face and the shiny metal balls of his piercings gliding through her watering mouth and rubbing the sides of her throat. *Oh god, yes. Take it, Mayan. Take it.* Gianna's mind went foggy, and her body went into autopilot, doing nothing but grasping his hand that was still around her throat and attempting to breathe around Mayan's thick dick.

She could hear Mayan's labored breathing through the fog as he spat out. "I've often wondered what you would look like with your mascara running while you gag on my dick." Releasing her throat, Mayan used both hands to crawl backward, removing himself from her mouth and bringing them face to face. Grabbing her throat and clutching at her chest, Gianna took in deep, drawn-out breaths. Wiping the slobber from her chin, he whispered, "You're more beautiful than I ever imagined."

In between breaths, she forced the words from her mouth. "Fuck. You."

As soon as the words were uttered, a sharp pain sprang to life in her nipple. Pinching hard enough to elicit a whimper from her, Mayan cooed, "Be a good girl, G."

Still holding the sensitive nub hard enough to make her entire body tense, he nuzzled his face tenderly into the crook of her neck, kissing it lightly. "Or I'll have to punish you." The sweet release of the pressure on her nipple made her suck in a breath of relief. His voice was deep and demanding, "Say sorry, G. Say sorry for being such an awful little brat."

Gianna's body was thrumming with anticipation. Her mind kept screaming, *Say it! Fucking say it. If that's the punishment, what the fuck is the reward?* But her heart desperately wanted to heal, wanted to reach out and heal his as well. Knowing things were about to get messy, Gianna moved her hand to her waistband.

Placing her lips gently on Mayan's, she pulled the gun out and raised it up above her head. She pulled away from the kiss, rolling her head back to see Stefan. His energy was clearly waning. The only part of him that was moving was his bobbing head as soft cries fell from his lips. Deciding to end his worthless life fast, Gianna squeezed the trigger, putting a bullet between his eyes. His head flung back, and blood sprayed the wall behind him before his head fell one last time.

Dropping the gun, Gianna brought a hand to Mayan's cheek and pushed the other under his shirt, bringing her fingertips to the jagged scar.

Watching his eyes close as he savored the intimate touch, the need to heal him grew. "I'm sorry, Mayan... I'm sorry he hurt us... I'm sorry I was so blind to your pain."

Mayan's hand pressed into hers, pushing it flat against the scar and holding it there. "Stop. Don't do this."

Her hand left his cheek, trailing down to his hand at his chest. Grasping his hand, she moved it from his chest to hers, laying it on her bare skin. "Please. Please, Mayan. I want to take your pain." She looked deep into his eyes, hoping he wouldn't reject her.

She didn't move or waver in the slightest as his eyes searched her face to find any semblance of uncertainty.

Not breaking eye contact, he sat up and moved back, bringing his knees to either side of hers, and unbuttoned her pants. She pushed at the pants, raising her ass up for him to pull them down further. The warmth of his hands caressed her bare hips as his eyes devoured the sight. Gianna's pulse quickened when he pulled out his knife and placed the cold steel against the heated skin of her thigh, just below her pink leopard g-string.

Tilting his head, he looked at her questioningly. "Are you sure you want this?"

She nodded eagerly, and in response, he swiftly cut the string. Letting the tip of the knife drag lightly across her clean-shaven mound, he moved to the other side. Keeping his eyes on the knife this time, he quietly asked, "Are you sure you want me?"

Dying to move but afraid he would stop, Gianna answered pleadingly. "Please, Mayan. Yes. I want you. I want this. Please."

The string fell to the floor under her, and she felt the cool air hit her warm, wet lips when he flipped the tiny patch of fabric down to the ground between her trembling thighs. Skin tingling with excitement and trepidation, Gianna watched in awe as he removed his pants, revealing well-toned muscular thighs and the full view of his impressively gorgeous package.

He lowered himself between her thighs, nudging her to widen for him. Gianna happily complied, wrapping her arms around his neck and pulling him down to her. He grabbed her face, and his mouth claimed hers in a kiss so possessive and all-consuming that, at that moment, she knew that the one and only thing she wanted, that she needed, was to be his. Forever.

His hand moved from her face to explore her body. She felt his thumb circle the still-tender nipple, stimulating it to a hard peek before moving further down.

His large hand cupped her fully, allowing her juices to wet his fingers as he rubbed his palm into her, making her clit sing with pleasure and cry with the need for more.

Overstimulated, Gianna grabbed his tight ass, digging her nails in while she pulled him into her. Mayan's fingers spread her lips, allowing the beaded head of his cock to kiss her begging clit. Moaning with pleasure, she begged him once more. "Please," she panted, then bit into his shoulder, making him growl between clenched teeth as he pulled away and brought the knife to her chest.

For a moment, she stopped breathing, his deep green eyes fixed on hers while his head lowered, bringing his lips to her neck. Placing soft kisses on her neck, he spoke, "Yours won't mean what mine does, G."

As the tip of the knife dove into her skin, just below the surface, Mayan pushed the head of his cock into her, just beyond the entrance.

Blood spilling out as fast as her tears, the knife continued down, slowly and deliberately torturing her. Still placing tiny, delicate kisses on her sweaty skin, he spoke softly, "This… is to remind you that you have always been mine. Even when you ran."

Mayan pulled back, leaving her empty and wanting. The knife lifted from her skin, bringing her mercy from the unbearable mixture of pleasure and pain that brought her to the edge of sanity.

Gianna's nails nearly pierced through the skin of her palms, before she released her clenched hands and took in a deep, steadying breath. *Breathe Gianna. Brea…*

Before she could finish her thought, the air was viciously sucked from her lungs as Mayan maliciously drove himself deep within her and swiftly sliced through her unprotected raw skin, completing the X she had begged him for and simultaneously causing her back to arch and her muscles to clamp down.

"This one… is so you don't forget that I will NEVER let you go again." Sucking in air through gritted teeth, the prison of pain gave way to toxic pleasures.

Having him buried deep within her, her mind began to focus on her clenching pussy that was eagerly attempting to pull him in deeper. She could feel every twitch, every throbbing pulse of his studded dick.

In an attempt to catch her breath, Gianna kept her back arched for a moment longer.

Because she knew that as soon as it returned to the floor, he would ravage her, breaking her in ways she couldn't even imagine.

The sweet sensation of his tongue tracing her ear made her pussy tighten around him. Releasing a moan of pleasure, her back began its descent.

As soon as the delicate skin of her back touched the floor, Mayan growled into her ear, sounding more beast than man. "I'll fuckin kill you if you try."

Dropping the knife to the floor, his arms curled beneath her arms, and his hands grasped her shoulders, pulling her onto his lap as he sat back.

Staring deep into her nearly onyx eyes, a slight smirk appeared on his face. "Now. Be a good girl and show me why I willingly gave you my soul."

Once again, in a position of power, the urge to take what she wanted and answer to no one came blazing back with a vengeance. Giving it everything she had, despite the open wound and the cock inside her, she punched that arrogant meathead right in his exquisitely square jaw.

Before he could react, Gianna cupped his face in both hands and tilted his head up to look her dead in the eyes.

"Why don't YOU show ME why I shouldn't piss on it and hand it back." Sudden and intense pain flashed like lightning through her as he brutally pinched both her nipples and pulled down, bringing her mouth so close to his that she could taste his sweet breath with every tiny inhale she could manage through the pathetic whimpers of pain that made his lap slick with her enjoyment.

Tugging down hard enough to bring her quivering lips to his after each word, he reprimanded her for her behavior.

"You. *tug* fuckin'. *tug* dirty. *tug* little. *tug* brat." With the last word, he brought her lips to his and did not let up as he spoke sternly with his lips on hers. "Say you're sorry… or I'll pull my fat dick out of your pretty little pussy right now."

Unwilling to call his bluff, Gianna widened her legs while reaching back to pull her cheeks apart to get every bit of him inside her that she could.

She began to raise herself up, and her eyes closed with the exquisite pleasure of each barbell popping out. Her voice jumped with each one while she apologized for misbehaving.

"I'm sorry, baby." Mayan's hands caressed her back and traveled to her shoulders.

With a groan of satisfaction, Mayan declared. "That's my good girl." Then grabbed her shoulders and pulled her down, driving himself into her. Gasping, Gianna's eyes sprung open at the sudden sensation of him bottoming out inside her.

Wrapping her hands around his neck and clasping them, she leaned back and began to grind against him in a circular motion. Mayan moved one hand to the small of her back, urging her to continue as she changed direction, swirling her hips to move him inside her and rubbing him against her G spot.

His other demonically possessed hand pressed the pad of his thumb down on her swollen clit. Matching her movements as she rode him, Mayan gently rubbed her. Panting heavily, Gianna stared into his eyes, watching him climb to the edge with her.

Pulling her closer, Mayan growled, "You gonna be my good girl and come for me? I feel you squeezing my dick harder and harder." Moving his thumb faster, he coaxed her closer to the edge with him. "Come for me."

Grabbing his muscled shoulders, Gianna dug her nails into his skin, answering him with her body while her mind swirled in ecstasy.

Eager to comply, her pussy began to quiver around him, and he swelled in response.

Mayan's hands were suddenly at her thighs. Forcing her down while he pushed up, Mayan moaned loudly as he began to come inside her.

The force of his warm cum shooting into her cervix as his cock swelled and twitched inside her shoved her off the cliff. Every muscle in her body clenched as the proof of her pleasure squirted out around his cock and began dripping down his thighs as she collapsed against him.

Hearts racing hard enough to feel them pounding, Gianna and Mayan stayed on the disgusting floor, cradling each other, with him still buried inside her.

She sat on top of him, his chest pressed to hers. She could feel the gentle rhythm of his heart, soothing her soul. She needed him. Her world was strange and not at all like she was led to believe it should be. But he was there, willing to hold her hand and walk beside her in her dark kingdom.

Her lips parted, and she quietly asked, "Is this what love is?"

The rough skin of his hand caressed her face as he brought his head back to look her in the eyes.

"Not all love is pretty, princess." His words curled around her black heart, making her eyes glisten with unshed tears as he wrapped his arms around her and pulled her close again. Covered in blood and cum with only a dead man to bear witness, Mayan whispered softly into her ear, "Marry me, G."

Chapter 7. Principe Demone

She said yes

With the woman of both his nightmares and dreams standing beside him, Mayan drifted off into thought as the iconic Elvis impersonator went through his spiel for the eighth time that night. *I thought for sure it would have taken more to convince her.* A giggle nearly escaped his lips when, *Yeah, but who wouldn't think marriage is a perfect way to end a night of murder, sex, dismemberment, and grave digging?* Went through his mind.

He squeezed her hand a little tighter when he realized that the memory of his perfect psycho princess wife insisting that they leave a few scrap pieces of meat near what she swore was a coyote den would forever be a favorite time to visit in his mind. *She's got a heart when it comes to animals.* He stopped and peeked at his future wife from the corner of his eye. *Animals like me... misfits that don't belong in a civilized world... predators.* He watched as her eyes shifted to him, and his chest tightened at the sparkle he hadn't seen in years.

She had tried to laugh off his proposal and even tried to talk her way out of it.

But the second he appeared to be ready to throw in the towel, she suddenly had a very practical reason for their marriage.

"I guess it's not an altogether terrible idea. It would give us a shot at spousal privilege if we ever needed it." The hesitant look of someone readying themselves for rejection was all he needed to know that she wanted it just as bad as he did. After cleaning themselves up, they rode into town. A few inquiries with some performers and a trip to the chapel shop for a black veil and their best tuxedo t-shirt because "Why the fuck not?" and they were at the altar. Ready to bind themselves to one another.

Stuck in his own world of recollection, the words, "I do," suddenly cascading from the most aggravating and seductive mouth he had ever known, stole any shred of humanity he had left. He would break any law, sever any bond, and cross any line to keep her, even if she begged him to leave. No divorce papers, judge, or order of protection would stop him. Nothing would keep him from buying a house in the country and burying her body under a majestic willow tree so he could keep her forever.

The turd brown eyes of the Elvis officiant fell on Mayan, and the words, "I do," flowed freely from his lips while the words *she's mine* burned in his mind.

Leaving behind an angry weeping wound that he knew would deepen and spread with time until it claimed every bit of him.

Turning to face his bride and seal the deal, he placed a finger under her chin, lifting her glossy eyes to his. "There is nowhere you could run that I wouldn't find you."

Smiling brightly at her husband's words, Gianna threw her arms around his thick, tattooed neck and kissed him deeply. After stealing his breath, he felt the sweet caress of her lips on his neck as she nuzzled him and whispered, "A little part of me wants to cut your Achilles tendon and lay you in my bed while you watch me put a bullet between the eyes of anyone who has ever looked at you." She released him and stepped back, placing her disinterested face back in place. "Only a tiny itty-bitty part."

Thankful the chapel had been close to the hotel, Mayan stepped out of the elevator, thoroughly exhausted. As they walked down the hallway side by side, Gianna threw her head back and groaned loudly, "I'm so tired! We should have waited for the wedding stuff."

Feeling a little slap-happy, he gave her ass a hard smack and enjoyed the small yelp it elicited from her as they approached their room. Before she could get mad, he stepped up to the room door and waved the key card before it. He made sure to give her a sly smile and wink as he opened the door for her to enter.

Following close behind her, he entered the room and immediately went to the side table where he had left his phone while they were taking care of Stefan. Scooping it up, he flopped down on the bed with a great harumph. He held it above his face and swiped up.

Three messages… Hmm, something tells me it's nothing good.

Message number one-

< Messages   Tanya   Details

> I know you typically don't want to hear about my "boy problems" but I kind of need you.

To which he promptly replied-

> You are correct. I don't get involved in your boy problems. So no, you don't need me.

> I also want to add that I've told you before, stop dating these punk-ass boys, and you won't have these problems

Text message number two-

●●●●   27% 🔋

< Messages   **Roman**   Details

> Just checking to make
> sure all is well. Meet me
> by the pool for a drink
> before you leave.

> Everything is taken care
> of. See you in the
> morning.

     The sudden sound of a melodious voice
beckoning him from the washroom pulled his
attention away from the last message before he
could respond to the third and final message.

> Poe ate all your fancy granola bars. I told him not to. But you know Poe. Once he sets his mind to something, there is no talking him out of it.

He would punch Nickels when he got home. Right now, his wife was calling him to shower with her before bed. *How adorably mundane,* he thought, as he walked toward the beautiful voice of his angel of death.

Steam billowed out of the bathroom as Mayan entered and hurried to disrobe. Moving the cheap white plastic curtain aside, he stepped in and was greeted with a wet, soapy embrace that turned him upside down. He had never felt the need to shower with someone or hold someone so close just to feel their heartbeat with his. It had always been about sex before this. But with her... For her... He wanted to hold her and chase away all her anger and self-doubt. For her, he wanted to take his time caring for her.

He would take the sponge and wash away her fears and stress while he memorized each dip, rise, curve, and line of her body.

But her hand on his engorged cock, running a finger along his excruciatingly tight piercings like a guitar string, told him that she had other plans. "Not right now, Principessa. Hand me the sponge and soap." He ran a hand down the slope of her back. "You need to be washed and put to bed."

A tiny groan of protest parted her lips before she spoke with her face still pressed against his chest. "I know what I need," she said, taking a firm hold of him.

In the blink of an eye, his softer side was pushed down while she lured the dominating bastard to the surface with her deliberate disobedience. Both his hands shot out at once. One grabbed her wrist, and the other her silky, slender throat. The black sleeve of tattoos on his arm flexed and wriggled as he raised her up to her tiptoes. He could see the fire dancing in her eyes as she spat into his face and tightened her grip.

She took short gasps of breath between struggling words, her grip tightening until her nails began to pinch his tender flesh. "I'll rip it off, you big dumb ape."

Ignoring her completely, Mayan closed his eyes and enjoyed every prick of pain with savage delight. *Fuck. I love her.*

Slowly, he opened his eyes to watch hers grow with panic. In a mocking tone, he declared, "No. You won't," as he continued to tighten his hand around her neck. Gianna's hand released his dick, and she used both hands in a feeble attempt to free herself. "Now… What you ARE going to do is clean the spit from my face. Then. You're going to hand me the sponge and soap like a good girl."

He stopped for a second to marvel at how beautiful her throat looked in his fist. "And if you don't want to listen, and you act like a disobedient bitch," His fist tightened, and his hand at her waist slid down her rounded ass to slip a finger between her cheeks. "I'll push your face down to the bottom of the tub and take that tight little ass of yours until you're sobbing and begging me to stop." He emphasized his point by pressing his finger against her pathetically puckered asshole. She could clench all she wanted. But it wouldn't stop him from teaching her a lesson if she needed it.

He brought his hand back to her waist, and he brushed a soft kiss across her lips. "Behave, and I'll clean my princess and lay her next to me for bed."

He ended by placing a feather-light kiss on her forehead, then released her throat, wrapping an arm around her at the same time to steady her as she greedily gulped in air.

Her breathing was still ragged, and her chest was rising and falling a little too fast when she did exactly what he expected her to do. She cocked her hand back and swung at his face. *That's my girl. Always a challenge.* Ready to show Gianna her place, Mayan caught her by the wrist before her open hand connected with his spit-covered face.

Crushing her dainty wrist within his rock-like fist, Mayan brought her hand across her body, spinning her in the dangerous dance she had so boldly asked for. Her wet slippery ass pressed into his hard shaft as he used his body to push her down to the ground.

She cried out as her knees banged against the floor of the tub. "Mayan!" Her hands began to frantically claw at anything they could. She tried to reach back to his thighs, and she even tried to push up. But her cries and struggles only excited him more.

He kept his body above her with his chest to her back to keep her from bucking, but his hand rushed to grip the nape of her neck. Her dark, wet locks spread across her beautiful face while he forced her cheek to the floor.

He stared down into her wild, wide eye while she panted through her open mouth. *She's a fuckin' angel.*

He used his other hand to grab his leaking dick and press the engorged head between her cheeks.

She squealed loudly at the contact and yelled, "I'm sorry!"

He froze, the water from the shower head pelting his face and shoulders. Was she really sorry? Or was this just a part of her game? Should he take her anyway?

Water sprayed from his lips as he ground out, "Last chance, G. Are you going to behave?"

Gianna's slippery body shook beneath him, and his cock ached to be inside her, feeling every bit of her anger grabbing and milking him while she fought.

Her lips moved awkwardly, almost like a fish. "I fucked up. I'm fuckin' sorry, Mayan." He felt her body go limp beneath him. "I'll behave."

He might regret it, but he believed her. He wrapped an arm around her waist and helped her up with him as he stood.

She turned within his embrace and raised her hand. He braced himself, ready for her to fight back again, but she didn't. She tenderly wiped the spit away, then turned and picked up the items he requested.

His heart beat hard in his chest as she turned back to place them in his hands. When she laid her head on his chest, he thought his heart might break through his ribcage. She was his fuckin' angel.

Happy that she didn't need more than a quick demonstration of how far he was willing to go to take care of her, he applied a generous glob of body wash to the sponge and began reverently washing every inch of her body. He stared at her beautifully bruised neck and finished on his knees before her as he washed her dainty feet.

He looked up at her and saw her powerfully shaped legs, perfect pussy, and her tight little tummy. For a moment, he stopped and stared. *I'm going to fill that tummy with my babies. That. Right there. That's where my babies will come from.*

Still dreamily thinking about the future and what it might hold, his eyes traveled to hers, and his brain turned to mush. Every poetic thought he had about her and her splendid body flew right out the window. Instead, he said, "You've got the best pigs I've ever seen, G."

Mayan continued to kneel and look into her smiling face while he ran the sponge over his body.

"Do you want me to wash you?" she asked quietly as she watched. In one fluid movement, he stood, set the sponge down, and grabbed the shampoo.

"No.," he said sternly while squirting it into his palm. "Turn around and tilt your head back." This wasn't about him. Sure, he was controlling her, but only to care for her. To show her how he would give her exactly what she needed, even if she hated him for it at first.

Looking like she was going to bite a hole through her lip, attempting to keep her mouth shut, Gianna did as she was told. Much to his surprise, she didn't utter a single word for the rest of their shower.

She just stared at him, almost like she had never had someone to take care of her. Realizing that she probably hadn't, just like he hadn't taken care of anyone before her, Mayan thought, *Stefan is lucky he's already dead.* Slapping some shampoo in his own hair and quickly rinsing it, his mind played through all the different ways he would kill that "man" if he had the power to continuously bring him back after each death.

Still daydreaming about rending every inch of skin from Stefan that had ever touched G, Mayan stepped out of the shower. "Stay in the warm water while I grab you a towel."

He was thankful that the neatly rolled towels were stored on a metal rack right above the toilet because as soon as his hand touched the towel, the shower stopped. *I knew she wouldn't behave for long.* Shaking his head, he laid the first towel on the floor, then quickly grabbed the second to wrap around his waist.

He knew exactly who his wife was, so he began to count down. *Three... Two...* As his fingertips touched the third towel, the curtain swooshed open dramatically, and Gianna stepped out, her arms crossed angrily over her wet breasts.

"I can get my own goddamn..." Before she could finish the sentence, he wrapped the towel around her and scooped her up. Cradling her in his arms as he walked her to the bed.

A smile split his face when he felt her nuzzle her head into his bare chest. She would always give him a fight, and he loved that about her. That's what made her submission that much sweeter. It would never last for long.

After gently sitting her on the bed, he walked around to the other side and removed the towel before crawling onto the bed and positioning himself behind her to dry her hair. Before he started, she leaned forward and grabbed her phone from the nightstand to check it while he worked.

Seconds later, her body tensed, and Mayan's curiosity got the better of him. "What's wrong?"

She shook her head and turned to face him. "I don't... It's just... I got an odd text from my father."

"I didn't even know he knew how to text." He shrugged. "So yeah, any text would seem weird," he said before laying the brush down and turning off the lamp on the nightstand. He laid back and pulled the blanket up to his chest. "What did it say?"

Gianna's weight shifted in the bed as she crawled under the blankets. Her leg wrapped around his, and she rested her head on his chest. The sudden light of the screen illuminated her face and stung his eyes as she read it out loud.

●●●   95% ▬▬▬

‹ Messages   **Papa**   Details

> Principessa, I'm sure
> you've already done
> what you need to do. I
> can always count on you
> doing what needs to be
> done. No matter what. I
> know I don't say it
> enough, or maybe at all,
> but I'm proud of the
> woman you've become. I
> love you, Papa."

He heard a soft sniffle. "There's another
one right after."

> P.S. Don't ever forget to
> check on your mother.
> She worries

Mayan's eyes were heavy with fatigue, but
before sleep claimed him, he did manage to say,
"I wouldn't worry. It sounds like a dad wanting
his daughter to know she's loved."

A long yawn refused to be subdued and interrupted him. He took the opportunity to squeeze her close, take her phone, and place it on the nightstand. "Old people tend to do that." His lips curled into a mischievous grin, and he sleepily said, "I'm sure I'll do it to our kids one day."

Morning came with more odd texts. Sitting up and swinging his feet over the side of the bed, Mayan grabbed his phone to check the time. "No way. Another from Roman?" he swiped up and opened the message.

●●●   100% ▬

‹ Messages   **Roman**   Details

Seriously. Please come down. We need to talk.

Be right down.

Thoroughly confused with absolutely no idea what he could want, Mayan left Gianna to sleep while he threw on some clothes and headed to the elevator. He didn't need to wake her up to figure out what it was his big brother needed now.

One elevator ride with a still drunk couple and a stroll through the lobby reassuring them he wasn't into a menage, and he was walking through the pool area with one hand in his pocket and the other shielding his eyes from the sun while he searched the tables.

Fuck... This better be good. I could be in bed with my wife right now. He smiled at the thought, but it fell quickly. *Are we letting the cat out of the bag? We didn't even talk about that.* His eyes finally landed on Roman, and he approached the table and then pulled out a chair to sit.

I'll wait to speak to G. Look at you. All good husband and shit already.

"You okay?" Roman asked, clearly concerned that Mayan hadn't said a word yet.

Attempting to stay present with Roman and not drift off into his honeymoon land, he cleared his throat and mind. "I'm good. What's going on?"

Roman sat back, took a few deep breaths, then began nodding. "Okay. So I'm a PI, right." Mayan's head was already nodding, and his hand was waving in a way that said to get on with it. "Well... I did some digging."

Mayan leaned forward, his brow knitting together. "What do you mean? On who? On what?"

Roman grabbed his hand in a gesture of love and reassurance that the boys rarely ever used. "Mom lied. Our father isn't dead."

Forget blown; Mayan's mind was absolutely demolished. He yanked his hand away and sat back. "Wow... What the fuck? They all lied to us?"

"It gets worse." Roman's eyes dropped to the ground. "Mom... umm, Lidia. Always wanted to have a baby with Regina. But obviously, that could never happen."

Mayan's brow furrowed, making deep creases appear on his forehead. "Duhh. So, they asked their friend Charles."

Roman nodded and nervously drummed his fingers on the table. "Right. That's what they told us. But that's not what happened. Liddia couldn't have a baby with Regina. BUT. She found a way to get as close as possible."

Anger spiked through him, tensing all his muscles. "Spit it out already."

"They asked Regina's brother to let Liddia use his sperm." Mayan sat there with his mouth open, and a look of utter disbelief plastered on his face. "Breathe, Mayan."

Once the words registered in his mind and he remembered his need for air, he took in a deep breath, then practically screamed, "Uncle Tony is our fucking father?"

Looking around with an overly apologetic face and waving at the people who were staring, Roman continued. "Listen. I was mad as hell when I found out, too. I even confronted him." He stopped waving and dropped his head into his hand. "That's why he and I don't get along anymore."

He rubbed his face hard, then looked up at Mayan and placed both hands on the table. "I told him I couldn't keep that from you, and he said it would only hurt you."
Anger bloomed on his face. "Hell. Even our parents said not to." Roman leaned back in his chair with a huff of disappointment. "I'm sorry, kid. I shouldn't have listened to them. I should have told you."

Mayan stood abruptly and raised an accusatory finger at Roman. "You're goddamn right you should have!" He bent down and slammed both hands on the metal table, making it rattle loudly.

At that moment, he was more vulnerable than he ever thought he could be, but he pushed through and asked, "Is that why you've been ignoring me?"

Roman replied truthfully and straight to the point. No pretty words to hide the cold truth. "Yes." The deep, profound pain of betrayal contorted his face, and Mayan stood and took two steps back. Roman stood and attempted to step around the table towards his brother with an outstretched hand. "I know it sounds weird... but I've been going to therapy."

Mayan stood there staring incredulously at what had to be an extraterrestrial being wearing a Roman suit. *Oh my god. Nickels is going to love this. Roman's been body snatched!*

Undaunted by his brother's blatant look of distrust, Roman continued.
"He says you need to let yourself feel and experience the feelings to get over them." He closed the gap between them. "Don't run away from it. Let yourself be mad, man."

Then, for the first and what he hoped wouldn't be the last time in his life, Mayan punched Roman right in the mouth. Time went into slow motion while he watched him fall back to the cement floor, then resumed normal pace as the onlookers started to rush over.

Before they could get to the pair, he put his hands on his hips and bent at the waist to stare down at Roman's split-open, bloodied lip for a moment. "How's that?"

"Great," Roman groaned, grabbing his back and shooing away concerned pool goers while Mayan strolled to the exit.

He swung open the door dramatically and walked out. But before the door closed, he popped his head back through and yelled, "You better hope you don't run into Nickels. Cause after I tell him what happened, he's going to want you to probe him."

Chapter 8. Principessa

Every beginning has an end

Sunlight peeking through the side of the heavy hotel curtains warmed Gianna's cheek. She kept her eyes closed as she began moving around in search of the big oaf, she had fallen asleep on. When she came up empty-handed, her eyes opened to narrow slits.

"Mayan?" Nothing. She called out again, this time louder. "Mayan! You in the bathroom?" Not garnering a response on her second try, she sat up and swiped her cell phone from the side table. *Clearly, he left me here while he went to play around in Vegas. Asshole.*

She opened her phone, and surprise and worry smacked her in the face. She forgot all about being angry with Mayan— twenty missed calls from her mother and two texts from Seppie.

●●●● 92% ▮▮▮

‹ Messages **Seppie** Details

Your mom is freaking out. She went coo-coo because Zio said she needed to get out of the house and sent her to a spa. Crazy old bat wouldn't go willingly, so Ralphy drove her. Apparently, she told him he had kidnapped her and even threatened to call the police. Obviously, he took her phone when she said that nonsense. Anyway, we left that tall new kid Jerry with her. He's supposed to make her spa appointments and make sure she stays away from phones. But you know her. She's spouting all kinds of crazy shit, trying to get someone to go get her. So if she happens to call you, ignore her. That's what I'm doing. I'm sure she will calm down by tomorrow.

●●●●   92% ▇▇▇▊

< Messages   **Seppie**   Details

> Let me know when you
> start the drive back.
> Can't wait to hear all
> about it, you psycho.

"What in the actual fuck is going on?" A
sudden vibration from her phone tickled her palm.
"Unknown number." She quickly pressed accept
and brought the phone to her ear. Disoriented,
screeching blasted through the speaker, and in an
effort to soothe her throbbing eardrum, she pulled
the phone a few inches away from her ear.

It was Teresa. "I don't know who's behind
it, but something is happening, Gianna.
Something big!"

"Whoa, whoa, calm down, Mama. What's
going on?"

"Don't tell me to calm down, dammit!
Something big is happening." Her voice lowered.
"They stuck me with that empty-headed Jerry kid.
I told him I got the runs from stress so I could
sneak out the other side of the bathroom." She
paused for a moment, then continued. "I don't
have long."

"Mom... I get it. Something big. But you're not telling me anything other than that."

In a soft whisper, she said, "It's your father, Gianna."

Irritated and wishing she would have listened to Seppie, she pressed her mother for more information. "Okay. What about him?"

A slight sniffle came through the phone. *Oh my god. Is she crying?*

"It started with his legs... he... he can't walk anymore." Gianna's shoulders slumped, and the only thing that she could think was *Fuck. No wonder why she's going crazy.* "The doctors. They say they can't help, and it's only going to get worse."

"Mom, I-"

Teresa interrupted, panic rising in her voice. "He wouldn't let me talk to them anymore. Wouldn't even tell me what it is."

Attempting to be the voice of reason and soothe her mother's nerves, she spoke calmly, even though she was just as concerned, if not more so. What would this mean for the Outfit? That kind of weakness displayed to our enemies, or those within seeking to overthrow, could have dire consequences. "Okay. I'm sure when I get home, we can figure this all out. He's probably just upset and needed some space."

She paused for a second. "You know, even though you mean well, sometimes, you can be a little much."

Big sobbing wails reverberated through her head. "No! He had me sign a bunch of crap and kept telling me how much he loves me." Teresa seemed to have an odd calm set in as she plainly said. "Then he had Ralphy carry me out while he yelled to me that he loved me and that you would take care of everything."

Terror gripped her heart, and her breathing began to speed up. Burning tears filled her eyes while the image of her father lying in bed, too weak and feeble to rise, took center stage in her mind. The sad, scared little girl inside her took a seat while the princess of darkness gave her a pat on the back and stepped forward. "I'll handle it, Mama. You enjoy your stay at the spa." Teresa resumed screaming while Gianna calmly placed her thumb on end.

She surveyed the room as if it wasn't empty and evenly stated, "Okay… get your shit… we gotta get home."

Gianna worked in a calculated, methodical manner to get everything she needed into her bags. She grabbed all her clothes and rolled them up neatly so she could make an even layer on the bottom.

Then she placed anything breakable on top and sandwiched it in between the bottom and another layer of clothes. Did she have to be so precise about her packing? No. But it did help her mind calm and give her hands something to do while she tried to figure out what the fuck was going on and how she was going to fix it.

Nearly done packing up her belongings, Gianna's steady rhythm was disrupted by Mayan's hulking frame stomping through the door. Refusing to look him in the face, she went back to organizing her neat bag. "I have to leave now. If you're coming, pack your shit, and fast." She lifted her eyes but did not meet his gaze; she didn't have enough control over her emotions. She looked down and fiddled with the different bottles of products. "His legs finally gave out. I'm pretty sure he's callin' it."

She flipped the flap down and zipped it closed, the zipper sounding like a chainsaw in the deathly quiet room. Her eyes began to sting again, but she wouldn't break now. *Fuck. I want to go back to not crying. How do people deal with this kind of nonsense? I got shit to do. I can't be crying.* She pulled the bag from the bed and began to walk to the door, but he stepped to the side, blocking her path.

His face was hard like stone, devoid of all emotion. "Are you saying he's going to off himself?"

Hearing it out loud made her legs weak, but she was the daughter of a Don; she wouldn't break easily. She straightened her back and plainly stated, "That. Or he's going to have Ralphy or Seppie do it." Placing her hands on his hard chest, she pushed hard, trying to make him step aside. When he didn't budge, she cleared her throat loudly. "Look, if you don't want to help me stop him, that's fine." Putting her full weight behind it, she rammed her shoulder into his brick-like chest. "But at least get the fuck out of my way!"

Vice-like hands grasped her shoulders and shook her so hard that her head bounced back and forth, making her teeth crash together painfully.

"Look at me!" He commanded in a menacing tone through gritted teeth. For a moment, she debated pulling out her gun and pistol whipping the stupid out of his thick skull. But there was no time for that.

Raising her eyes, she searched his face. His jaw was tense, and worry lines marred what was otherwise typically smooth. Clear evidence of genuine concern. His hands moved to cup her face, and he brought his forehead to hers.

Staring deep into her watery eyes, he said, "I will never leave your side. Do you understand me?" One almost unnoticeable bob of her head was all she could muster as a response. "We stand together, and we fall together. Nothing else matters." His lips pressed gently onto hers, and he pulled her into his protective embrace.

Without much thought, Mayan and Gianna boarded the first flight they could get home. They were thankful to have found that luck was on their side, and they didn't complain about separate seats on the flight that left within the hour. Both had their world perched precariously on their shoulders, with few options to keep it from crashing.

After a less than stellar takeoff during which they circled the runway more times than she had ever seen a plane do, Gianna leaned her head against the window and closed her eyes.

The two women seated beside her didn't seem to care that she was obviously looking for some quiet. A rail-thin woman with brown highlighted hair swooped up in a messy bun, sat beside Gianna. Next to her, was a carbon copy, except her hair was blonde with lowlights.

"I agree, Carol, I've tried it, and it's delicious. Tim must be out of his mind."

The one sitting next to Gianna must have been Carol because she replied, "I know, Karen. My own husband was telling me I'm not making my lasagna right." She huffed, and Gianna felt a light nudge of a bony elbow knock into her shoulder as the woman crossed her arms. "I know it's better with Greek yogurt." Gianna's lip curled, and her nostrils flared. *Her husband is right.*

Gianna accepted she wouldn't be quieting her mind any time soon when the two women immediately vaulted into another conversation. Sitting up, she pulled out her cell phone and logged into the airline's Wi-Fi. *At least Seppie and I have iPhones. I can send him an iMessage.*

✈ 94% ▬

‹ Messages **Seppie** Details

> Yeah, she called. She is really going overboard this time. I don't have the energy or the time to entertain her today. Dumbbell for brains insists we leave today.

Nice. When you get back, I'll stop by your place, and we can talk about your trip.

> Why didn't you tell me Papa gave Mayan the scar?

Whoa. What? Where the hell did this come from?

> I know you knew Seppie. You know all the dirty little secrets. Don't fuckin' lie.

Hey! Don't call me a fuckin' liar. I didn't lie. I didn't say I didn't know. I asked where this is coming from. A few days with Meatwad in the lotus, and you suddenly give a shit?

Gianna gripped her phone tightly as she read the message and felt her eye twitch.

> I didn't think you would have kept that from me. That's all. Out of everyone in my life. I have trusted you the most.

She wasn't surprised when he didn't respond.

FUCK, the lotus!

Gianna sat up and unbuckled her seat belt while scanning the plane to find Mayan again. He was three rows ahead of her. In the middle seat, sandwiched between what looked like a straight-laced businessman typing on his laptop and your average Joe in a flannel.

Adjusting herself to face towards the aisle, she cleared her throat, interrupting the gossip girls. "Excuse me. I need to get through."

Carol glared up at Gianna as she stood. "You know the seatbelt sign is still on, right?"

Gianna's eyes narrowed, and she had to hold herself back from stomping her heel into the bitchy woman's thigh. After a deep breath, she pushed through the woman's legs with a nasty little smirk. "That's nice, now move."

After stumbling out into the aisle, she straightened her pants and walked to where Mayan was seated. Undaunted by the women bitching like clucking hens behind her.

As she approached and saw his face, she realized, *This mother fucker is sleeping.*

She smiled politely at the bald man in flannel and poked Mayan's shoulder. With a small snort, his eyes opened, and he looked around.

His eyes settled on Gianna, crossing her arms and tapping her foot. "What's up?" He asked sleepily.

"I was sitting there with Wingus and Dingus." She stopped and hiked her thumb toward her seat. "And I wondered. What the hell are you going to do about the Lotus?"

Mayan's eyes rolled, and he sighed loudly before closing his eyes again and crossing his arms. "I took care of it. Roman and Lyla are driving her back." He sunk down in his seat. "Now go sit down."

Her muscles tensed, and she wanted to reach over and smack him before she left. But she didn't. She turned around and walked back to her seat, where her new besties waited with bitchy glares.

It only took a few minutes, and Gianna was anxiously fiddling with her phone. Debating if she should get up again. The conversation beside her made the decision for her.

"Scotty is so good at tap. You wouldn't believe it. Tasha absolutely loathes us because of his talent."

"I'm not surprised she's jealous of your son's skills. Her son can barely walk without tripping."

Holy fuck. No. I'm not listening to this crap. This time, she didn't even ask. She simply stood and pushed through. She was pretty sure she heard, "I'm getting the flight attendant." while she walked to Mayan again.

This time, she didn't even smile at the flannel nobody. She launched right into talking.

"Mayan."

His eyebrows jumped, but he didn't open his eyes. "Hmm?"

She asked her question, with thinly veiled anger, through gritted teeth. "How are we getting to my parent's house?"

Again, his eyes didn't open. She was getting really sick of his shit.

"Dante and Nickels are picking us up at the airport." She turned and walked back to her seat. She ignored the huffing women while she shimmied to her seat and continued to fight with Mayan in her head. *When the fuck did he text them? And why didn't he tell me? Like I don't need to be involved? Who the fuck does he think he is?*

Gianna put her hand to her forehead and slumped down in her seat. She was exhausted. Her brain was running a million miles an hour.

Her inner voice chastised her. *Why the fuck didn't you think of any of this any other fuckin' time Gianna? Making Mayan look at the guy who was dressed exactly like where is Waldo in the airport was more important. Not a chance, idiota. Get up and make sure you have what you need.*

She stood and grabbed the back of the seat in front of her while she looked at Mayan. He wasn't sleeping anymore. He had his phone up. *What the fuck is he doing? Who is he texting?* She stopped for a moment and felt a little foolish. *I guess I could have texted him and asked this stuff.*

But then she thought of a way that it would still be his fault. *To be fair, I didn't know he had turned on the Wi-Fi. He certainly didn't do it to text me.* Anger ran through her mind like bolts of lightning, and her dark gaze fell to the women next to her.

Carol peered up at her. "Ugh. Again? Seriously, this is ridiculous."

Gianna bent down so she was a few inches from the woman's face. "Get the fuck out of my way." Carol went to speak, but Gianna put a finger to her lips. "Stop talking, or when we get off this plane, I'll follow you to whatever suburban shithole you live in and slit your throat on your front lawn."

She looked at Karen, daring her to say a word, and then back to Carol. "And your friend's a fucking liar, your husband is right." She raised her voice, not quite yelling but louder. "Your lasagna sounds disgusting!" With their legs to the side and their mouths hanging open, Gianna walked through easily. She was ready to fuck up Mayan now.

She didn't smile at him, and she didn't ignore him. She bent down and looked flannel jackass in the face. "Are you from Chicago? Or the burbs?"

Mayan looked at Gianna, his phone in his hand. She watched as it lit up with a text that read Tanya. "What the hell are you doing?" She didn't answer him. She just stared, waiting for an answer.

The confused man looked at her warily. "Chicago."

Her smile grew. "So you have probably heard of the La Rosa's." He nodded slowly.

She stuck her hand out. "Nice to meet you, I'm Gianna La Rosa." His eyes grew wide, and his hand shook as he reached for hers and shook it firmly. "Get up. You have to use the washroom." Without a word, he unbuckled his seatbelt and went on his way.

Gianna sat down next to Mayan and cupped his face. Bringing her lips to his ear, she whispered in a low sultry voice. "You have three seconds to tell me what whore you're texting. Or I swear I'll open the emergency exit door and push you out while the plane plummets toward the ground." Then she slapped his cheek and sat back, crossing her arms while she waited for his response.

"Jesus, G." Mayan's stern face softened, and he laughed. "It's my little cousin, Tanya. You want to see?" He swiped his phone open. As her eyes scanned the phone, he leaned over and kissed her cheek. "I love you, you psycho bitch."

Her cheeks grew hot while she read.

✈   63% 🔋

‹ Messages   **Tanya**   Details

> I know! I know I shouldn't let him walk all over me. But I mean… I'm not that girl, My My. I can't seem to open my mouth when he yells or walks away with my shit.

> I'm going to send someone if he doesn't stop Tanya, whether you like it or not.

> He will. I swear.

She looked away from the phone instead of apologizing or discussing it further. Then said, "I... Umm... Just wanted to know if they'll have everything we need." She tucked her hair behind her ear. "I don't want to be driving around."

He put his arm around her shoulders and pushed her head onto his shoulder. "I told you. I took care of everything."

A content feeling spread through her. Right before he pushed her head away from him. "Now get back to your seat and stop making a damn scene." Gianna sat there in utter disbelief. A finger tapped her shoulder, and she jumped.

It was the flannel dude. "Umm, do you want me to sit in your seat?"

She shook her head and stood, saying, "No, you sit next to this asshole." Then she stomped down the aisle back to her quiet row and sat.

That was the last trip she made to him. For the rest of the flight, every time she thought of a question, she thought to herself, *I would set myself on fire and beg a priest to pull out his dick and piss on the flames before I would do that again.*

Gianna exited the plane, still highly irritated with him. After being trapped for the remainder of the flight with her own thoughts, she kept a brisk pace as they made their way to the pickup area.

He attempted to get her to slow down a few times. He called out her name in anger from a few people behind her more than once. With each one she ignored, her smile grew a little bigger.

By the time they made it out of the building and found the car, Mayan had had enough. When she reached for the handle of the back passenger side door, his hand slapped loudly against the window, closing the door.

His head lowered to her ear, and his voice was quiet and patient. "I know you're hurting. And I'm okay with you passing that pain to me." His hand left the window and laid atop her own on the handle. "But I need you to remember. I'm not the enemy."

Closing her eyes to collect herself and keep the tears from forming, she took in a ragged breath. "I... I know." His fingers curled around her own and pulled up on the handle. The door opened, and she slid inside the pearl white escalade, pulling her bag into her lap.

She didn't meet Dante's eyes when he turned to greet her.

"Umm... Hey, G." He rubbed the back of his neck nervously. "It's umm, been a while since we were all together like this," he said uncomfortably. Her mouth opened, but no words would come.

She clamped her mouth shut in embarrassment and gave a small smile and nod of her head instead. Dante turned away, and she felt her stomach sink. *You're not this weak. You have a voice, Gianna!*

She leaned forward and called out to him. "Dante."

He turned back and looked at her, his hand on the headrest of the passenger seat. "Yeah, G?"

"Thank you." She looked down and nervously wrung her hands. "For coming and helping me."

"G," he said. She looked up into his soft brown eyes. "There was never a time we wouldn't have come to help you if you would have let us." And with that, he turned back. Gianna slumped back in her seat, unsure about the tornado of emotions she was caught in.

With a mouth full of food, Nickels spoke loudly from beside her, breaking the tense moment. "Want a fancy granola bar?" He presented one proudly, then spoke in a conspiratorial whisper. "Dante said not to talk. Shhhh. These are for Mayan from Poe... but we can have some... poe said so." He winked at her and eagerly waited for her response.

The passenger door swung open, and the car rocked slightly when Mayan sat in the seat and slammed the door.

Getting right down to business, he turned to Dante. "You bring everything we need?"

Dante mindfully pulled away from the curb and into the flow of traffic as he replied, "Of course I did."

His head swiveled from side to side while he weaved in and out of cars as though he had done it a million times before and was just on repeat. "I got a few pistols and the knives you requested from under your pillow."
He looked at Mayan with his eyebrows raised. "You know that's fuckin weird, right?"

Nickels's brow furrowed. "You mean you don't?"

Dante looked at his brother in the rearview mirror incredulously. "Of course I don't. I'm not that fuckin' weird."

Gianna felt Nickels's elbow bump into her bicep. "You got knives under your pillow? Maybe a gun?" He sat there staring at her, waiting for a response.

"Well... Yeah. I mean. No knife. But I do keep my little Beretta under my pillow."

Gianna's eyes widened, and she flinched back as Nickels turned towards the front and exclaimed loudly. "HA! You lose Dante." Dante shook his head but said nothing. He just continued to navigate between cars.

"If three out of four have some kind of weapon under their pillows, then wouldn't it be odder NOT to have one?" He laughed and nudged Gianna. "Right? I'm right, right?"

He rolled his eyes and sat back while crossing his arms triumphantly. "That's math, my good man. Undisputable."

He leaned towards Gianna and whispered loudly. "Nothing has changed since you went all Casper. He's still more muscle than brain." he said, tapping a finger to his head.
"But Mama Dante means well. Telling us we shouldn't run with knives and such." He jutted his chin out and smiled a big toothy smile at his brother. "Don't ya, Dante?"

Dante's face was now red with fury, and Mayan chuckled while nodding his agreement with Nickels.

Dante smoothed his hair back and exhaled loudly, appearing to try to calm himself. "Whatever…" He looked at all of them one by one. Under his breath, he mumbled, "Assholes."

She looked around the car and suddenly realized why her childhood home hadn't been her home in so long. The reason why her apartment had never felt like it, either. They had become her home after Roman introduced her. Without them, she was alone in the world. Gianna had finally come home.

Dante cleared his throat, then glanced at Mayan. "Soooo, are you going to tell me where we're going AND WHY?"

As the conversation took a severe turn down the minefield that was her life currently, Gianna couldn't bear to listen. Instead, she lost herself in thought while gazing at the colors the sinking sun painted the sky with.

The look of unparalleled shock on Ralphy's face when the front door burst open under the pressure of Mayan's colossal kick, while Gianna strode through confidently with her gun trained on the spot directly between his eyes, would stick with the four reunited friends for the rest of their lives.

Ralphy sat back in the wingback chair, while Gianna stood just a few feet away with Mayan, Dante, and Nickels spread out behind her. Her eyes narrowed. "Who's with him, Ralphy?"

Raising his hands calmly, he attempted to defuse the situation "Gianna, you know you can't do this." He looked toward her father's bedroom and then back to her. "It's what he wants."

Grinding her teeth together, she gripped her gun harder, her knuckles whitening. "Dante. Stay with Ralphy."

"You got it, G." Dante nodded his head at the stone man with his gun pointed at him. "Hey, Ralphy. How you been?" He shrugged and gave an odd half-smile. "Sorry about this. You know how those La Rosa's can be hotheads."

Ralphy shrugged back and nodded his head while raising his eyebrows. "Don't I know it?"

Ignoring the men who were talking like no one had any guns pointed at anyone. She made her way to her parents' bedroom with long, confident strides—well, as long as her legs went anyway. This time, as she walked through their home, she didn't wonder about her place in it. And she certainly didn't wonder about her parentage.

She realized that her fierce love, which bordered on crazy, came from her mother. Teresa was willing to call everyone and anyone like a lunatic to save him.

She may not be exactly like her mother, but she was just as stubborn and set in her ways. Their houses may not look the same, but they were their own, and no one else would tell them how to keep them.

Mayan and Nickels stood behind her as she grasped the handle, turned, and pushed the French doors open.

To her absolute horror, Seppie stood beside the bed her father could no longer leave on his own. Seppie's hand lay on the pillow beside his head, holding a cocked gun. Blood pounding in her ears, she bellowed, "Step back, Seppie!" Her cousin's face turned to her, and she saw the tears streaming down his cheeks.

"I can't. He's already drugged." He took in a ragged breath. "He won't feel it, Gianna. He wants it this way." A sob claimed his voice, and Gianna's lip curled in disgust. "He doesn't want to go out a withered shell." His hand gripped his shirt over his heart. "I don't want to... I don't! But who am I to deny him?" He threw his hand out and yelled, his face red and the veins in his neck popping, "WHO?"

With cold indifference, she waved her gun to the side, gesturing for him to step back. "If you pull that trigger, two girls will lose their father tonight."

Her tone dripped with venom. "Because if you pull that trigger, I'll kill you." He tried to interrupt her, but she spoke louder. "If you don't leave this room, I'll kill you." His mouth shut. "Because you're my favorite cousin, you have four seconds to go sit out there with Nickels." Her head tilted to the side, and a brow popped up. "Or I kill you."

"Gianna! He wants this for you. He said him being sick would make you too weak to take control." He looked into her eyes, now deep black pits of death, beseechingly. "Please, Cugina. Understand."

"One."

His eyes darted to Mayan, who was now standing beside her, and he pleaded. "You have to understand!
"

"Two."

A whistle echoed into the room from just beyond the threshold. Nickels poked his head in. "Come on, boy. Let's go."

He continued in a loud whisper. "I think she's serious." Then he gave Seppie a big smile and took something from his pocket.

"Look, man. I have this fancy-ass granola bar I'll even share with you."

"Three."

Seppie's hand finally left the gun on the pillow, and he brought both up to cover his face and mouth. Pain-filled sobs leaked through his hands as he stumbled out of the door and into Nickels's oddly comforting embrace.

"See, buddy. I give little baby grandma hugs. They're good, right?"

Gianna didn't blink or move an inch until the doors clicked shut behind her. And as though someone had pulled a rug out from beneath her feet, she fell to her knees. The pain of her kneecaps bouncing on the wood floor didn't even register as she sat there blankly, staring at her father's chest. She watched it rising and falling with bated breath. As though any second now, it would be his last.

Her eyes moved to his face, and her heart squeezed. *He looks so feeble. So fragile. How did I not see this? I was only gone for three days.* Having her father so close to death forced Gianna to truly see him.

The invincible supervillain she had always seen when she looked at her father had been a memory. In her mind, he had stopped aging long ago. And in this moment, all the years crashed into him at once.

She couldn't be sure how much time had passed before the gentle caress of Mayan's hand on hers jolted her out of the trance-like state. He was kneeling beside her.

She nodded her head towards the bed. "That's his favorite suit."

"Yeah? I could see why. He does look nice in it."

A chuckle slipped past her lips, and she brought the back of her hand to her nose, wiping away the little dribble of fluid leaking from it. "Actually. He thinks he looks like a shmuck in it. It's Mama who says it's her favorite." Giving her best impression of Teresa's nasally thick Chicago accent, she mimicked her mother. "Oh, Geo. What are you after? Coming out here in that. You know what seeing you all distinguished and refined does to me."

With a look of complete understanding, he nodded. "He wore it for her."

She turned to him, her voice uneven and small, "He may be a heartless bastard, but only because he gave it to her."

The corner of his mouth tipped up, and he bumped her shoulder with his. "I know the feeling." Her eyes returned to her father. "It's not too late, G. We can call an ambulance. Have his stomach pumped."

A low groan rumbled from Geo's chest, and Gianna's head whipped in his direction. She rose to her feet with a humorless laugh and walked to his closet. She turned on the lights and disappeared from the world.

Their closet had always been divided. It occurred to her that until today she never cared to look at her father's side.

She ran her hand along the hanging clothes as she walked. Certain shirts jumped out at her and threw her into a memory of the last time he wore it. Some were just him in his office, others on important holidays. She stopped suddenly. It felt as though her feet had become rooted to the ground.

With her hand on the hanger, she pushed to reveal the writing "World's best farter." She had given it to him for Father's Day to make him mad. But he wasn't mad when he opened it; he smiled at her, set his cigar in the ashtray, and swapped the shirts. Much to her surprise, he wore it the entire day and made everyone laugh when they saw him.

Oh, Papa, I guess there were little moments of sunshine. She dropped her hand and walked to the back of the closet where his dresser was. She opened the top drawer where he kept his best cigars. The Cubans.

When she reemerged, Mayan was where she had left him. She looked down at the box of Cubans, cutters, and matches, then back to Mayan.

"I'm sure whatever they gave him was just something to make him sleepy and loopy."

She gestured towards him with the box. "Can you help me with this?"

He rose from his knees and walked across the room. Taking the items from her, he ran his hand across the top of the box. "Are you sure?"

"Yeah. I think he would like it." She patted him on the shoulder and walked past him. "I'm going to talk to my dad."

Each step was harder than the last. As she approached, small groans and indecipherable whispers found their way to her ears and made her heart want to shred its way through her chest. With more compassion than she ever thought she could have for the man who shot her, she began stroking Geo's hair lovingly. Gianna's hand went over his heart, and she bent to bring her face closer to his. "Papa…" she said, giving him a shake on his chest.

"Papa." His eyes lazily opened to slits and made an almost croaking sound.

She cleared her suddenly thick throat, and his bloodshot eyes slowly traveled to her. They scanned her face. "I'm here, Papa. I need you to know that I'm here to make you proud." His hand slid off his stomach and moved to cover hers. "I'm sending you. Not Ralphy. Not Seppie. Me," she said with finality.

The warmth of Mayan's arm comforted her as it grazed hers. He came up beside her and waved the lit cigar before Geo's face. "Hey there, boss. How's about a puff?"

Giovanni's outstretched lips were all the confirmation he required. Accepting the cigar Mayan placed between his lips, Geo took a long drag, then exhaled. Smoke rolled from his mouth and across his chest.

A reluctant smile appeared on Mayan's face as he brought the cigar away from his mouth. "Well, you did it. You got old and fat." His eyes closed, and he shook his head as he laughed softly. "You know, the good stuff." The corner of Geo's mouth tipped up for just a second, and then Mayan took a few steps back and wrapped his strong arms around Gianna, placing the cigar in one hand and the small, silenced pistol on the pillow.

His lips settled on her cheek in a comforting kiss that lingered. As they stood there, time slowed for her. She felt her father's heart beating beneath her hand and Mayan's against her back. Giovanni could be a cold man, and when his temper flared, he often did things he regretted, but he still had a heart. And he had failed when he tried to destroy Mayan's heart all those years ago. And still. Mayan was still here for him. Here for her.

The warmth of his body left her, and she knew it was time—time to be the monster the Don had raised her to be. His hand tightly squeezed hers, and their eyes locked.

A cracking whisper fell from his lips, "I love you, baby."

And just like that, all the ugly was gone. Washed away by every tender moment between them flashing before her eyes. Every goodnight kiss, tuck-in, and piggyback ride—all the top-secret midnight popsicles. And even the time he kept her home from school and let her ride with him for the day around the city. Showing her that a true Don is a part of his city. Not above it.

It was at that moment that Gianna La Rosa, daughter of the Don, and underboss of the Chicago Outfit, broke.

Raging rivers of tears streamed down her face, and through blurry eyes, she raised the cigar in an unsteady hand to his dry lips. He bit down and closed his eyes while she stroked his hair again.

After a moment, she gained the courage to ask, "Do you remember the song you would sing to me before bed?" A tiny, almost indiscernible nod of his head and her hand moved to hold his. She started to sing. She was off-key, and her voice was cracking, but none of that mattered.

"You are my sunshine. My only sunshine. When you're not happy." Her voice broke with a sob when he began to hum along. "My skies are grey." Looking down at her father a small sad smile appeared on her face. "You'll never know dear; how much I love you."

She stopped singing, and he continued to hum. Gianna bent lower to kiss his cheek before she whispered, "I married the Principe." Her quivering lips kissed his forehead for the last time before she continued to sing.

"Please don't take my sunshine away." Her voice didn't' crack, and she didn't waver in the slightest as she said, "I love you, Papa; good night." Then she squeezed his hand, and the trigger.

At nine p.m. CST, Giovanni La Rosa, Don of the Chicago Outfit, died, humming You Are My Sunshine to his daughter, the queen, with her king beside her, a cigar between his teeth, a smile on his face, and on his own terms.

Bonus chapter

(*giggles and whispers under breath, boner chapter)

The cool morning wind blew through Gianna's soft hair into Mayans face. As his arms encircled her from behind the scent of oranges and mint filled his nose calming his nerves. He hadn't been able to be with Gianna since Geo's death. She had been staying with her mother and Seppie.

They had only texted while she was keeping Teresa calm and helping with the funeral arrangements. Even though he knew there was a good reason for it, he hated every second of it.

He brought his hand up to her cheek and wiped the tear he knew he would find there. "I love you, G."

She turned in his arms and pressed her face into his chest, hiding away from the world. "Take me home, Mayan."

"Okay, princess, let's go say goodbye to Giuseppe and your mother." He slid a finger under her chin and lifted her face to look into her eyes. "Then I'll take you anywhere you want."

She gave a small nod and walked the few steps to the front of her father's mausoleum. Her mother, Seppie, and Ralphie stood before the door thanking the long line of mourners for coming. Mayan refused to let go of her hand as she slid behind her mother and placed a gentle hand on her shoulder. "I need to leave Mama."

Teresa's head turned towards her, her eyes sad and face pinched with concern. Gianna reassured her mother. "I'll call you later."

Seppie leaned in and whispered, "Zia, you keep the line moving. I'll talk to G." Teresa smiled weakly and turned back to the mourner. The three of them walked around to the back, and Seppie immediately embraced G in a hard, rib-crushing bear hug. After a moment, he released her and wiped a tear from his eye. "Go. Get out of here." He waved his hand towards the cars. "You need to get away from all this. I'll take care of everything here"

Mayan smiled and shook Guiseppie's hand. "Thanks, man." Guiseppie pat Mayan on the back and pushed them away from the building. "Make sure you take some of those bags of cookies from the car." Gianna rolled her eyes at him while shaking her head. "Seriously, G, we baked so many cookies with Zia. I can't take them all home."

Mayan turned to Gianna with a raised eyebrow as they walked. "Cookies?"
Gianna smiled as she wrapped her arms around herself. "My mom was having such a hard time. We didn't know what to do." A small laugh escaped her. "Next thing I knew, Seppie had a huge bag of flour, and he insisted we find out how many cookies it could make."

Mayan opened the door to the lotus for Gianna and took her delicate hand as she sat. "So, how many did it make?" he asked as he closed the door.

He ran his hand across the hood as he walked to the driver's side. *Cookies. Gianna La Rosa makes cookies.* His head shook, and a playful smile spread across his face. *I honestly didn't think she could cook. What a relief.* He slid into the driver's seat and started the engine. "So. How many did it make?"

Gianna's voice was small, and he almost didn't hear her as they drove out of the cemetery. "I don't know. I stopped counting after one hundred."

He laced his fingers through hers and brought her hand up to place a gentle kiss on her knuckles. As he turned onto the main road, his brow furrowed. "Umm, G, you said you wanted to go home, right?"

She looked at him questioningly. "Yeah?"

He pursed his lips and then sucked his tooth. "Where exactly is it that we have decided we are calling home?"

He felt her hand tense in his. "Umm. I don't know. I guess we could try my place." Mayan nodded his head, but inside, he was freaking the fuck out. *Her place? I'm supposed to go to her apartment and sleep there. Okay, Mayan. Calm down. You are acting like a scared little bitch.* He let out a long, drawn-out breath and hissed, "Great." under his breath.

His hands held her hips possessively as she opened her apartment door and walked in, flipping on the lights and revealing the sparse area. His eyes widened, and his shoulders became rigid.

She pushed his hands away from her hips, and he was in such a state of shock they simply fell to his side. She began walking around showing him all the nothing. "This is the kitchen. That's the umm." she waved a hand towards what he assumed would be the living room. "Well. You get it." She shook her head, went into a door to their left, turned on the lights, and yelled out to him, "Mayan. Come on. This is the bedroom."

His lip curled up as he walked in and saw the king-sized bed and one side table. There was no way he was going to do this. With calm, measured steps, he walked up behind her and grabbed her by the hips. She pushed back into him immediately, rubbing her plump ass onto his crotch. He bit back a growl, and threw her over his shoulder, ignoring her questions and demands while he walked back out of the apartment, making sure to turn off all the lights as he went.

Unceremoniously plopping her down in front of the elevator, he calmly said, "Shut your mouth, G." He watched her face as it twisted from confusion to outrage and knew she wasn't going to be listening to him. He raced to speak as she sputtered incoherently. "I'm not staying there. That isn't a home, G, it's weird and empty." He put his hands on her shoulders and brought his face down to hers. Her mouth was open, but she just stood there staring at him as though she was a frozen computer screen. "Let's go to my place, princess, I'll take care of you there."

He ran his knuckles down the side of her face. "I'll even cook."

She pushed her fist into his chest. "Fuck you, Mayan." Crossing her arms over her chest, she turned away from him. "There's nothing wrong with my apartment, asshole."

God, she's adorable when she pouts.

"You're right, baby. There's nothing wrong with your apartment." He pulled her back to his chest, and she reluctantly let him. "It's me. I need my stuff."

She looked at him incredulously. "You'll cook?"

Reaching past her, he pressed the call button for the elevator. "Yeah, I'll cook," he said confidently, as he shuffled her into the elevator. *More like Dante will cook.* He pulled out his phone and sent the guys a warning in the group text.

●●●● 18% 🔋

< Messages **Chuckle Fucks** Details

> I'm bringing G home.
> Pick up and make the
> place presentable,
> dammit. Don't let her
> take me back to her
> place. I can't do it. I
> won't. Nickels, no weird
> shit. Dante, start cooking
> something good.

Dante

The Ice castle can't be
that bad.

Nickels

Weird shit... Got it!

> You have no idea. I'll
> explain later. Just hurry
> up and make something.

Nickels

Is it barbies? I bet it's
barbies and weird dead
body tea parties!

Tell G I want a sleepover!

After an extremely uncomfortable, loud drive to his apartment, Mayan had finally convinced Gianna to try staying at his place for at least one night. He had to bargain with her, though. He had to agree to go to her place the next night. Gianna stepped out of the Lotus and walked to the front of his building.

She stopped before it and looked up. "Mine's better."

Mayan laughed as he walked up beside her. "Calm down. You'll love it. I promise."

She looked at him from the corner of her eye and crossed her arms. "Deals off.

"What!? You can't do that, G. We are already here."

She tapped her heel on the sidewalk and a finger to her chin. "Okay. BUT. I want one more thing."

Looking at the smile on her face, Mayan's gut churned. *What's the evil bitch brewing?* He crossed his arms and tried to appear relaxed. "And what's that?"

She turned to him and looked down at her shoe, then back up to him. "Lick it."

He laughed heartily, his shoulders bobbing as he grabbed his stomach. "Hell no. I'll just carry you up."

"You touch me, and I'll scream." She smiled sweetly at him. "Try me."
He searched her face for any sign of humor but found only smug resolve.

Closing his eyes he licked his lips and raised his hands in surrender. "Okay, okay," he said. He opened his eyes and slowly dragged his gaze from her toes to her eyes, following every dip and curve as though he were caressing her.

He watched as her face changed from cool arrogance to unsure arousal. The corner of his lip curled into a smirk. "Anything to make you happy, princess."

Uncaring of the watchful eyes of the world around them, Mayan lowered himself to his knees before her. He wrapped his fingers around her ankle and savored the warmth of her skin beneath her sheer black stockings.

Excited anticipation danced on his skin as he brought her heel to his face and raised his burning green eyes to stare into hers, with something that could almost be mistaken for innocence playing on his face.

Opening his mouth, he watched as her eyes widened and her lips parted on a sharp inhale. His cock pulsed hard against his thigh as her chest rose higher and fell hard. "Just remember, G. Everything has a price. Even happiness," he said as he inserted the heel into his mouth. He slowly pulled it back out with an obnoxiously loud sucking noise.

Releasing her foot, he stood and wiped his knees while she turned away with a huff and walked to the apartment building door.
His arm brushed her shoulder as he slid up behind her and reached past her to open the door.

She looked over her shoulder at him before entering and mumbled, "I only said to lick it, you sick bitch." Her hair brushed against his face when she turned back, the scent of her shampoo momentarily distracting him. She was only able to take one step before his hand was wrapped around her neck, and he was pushing her back against his hard chest.

Gliding his lower lip around the edge of her ear, he growled, "I did it. But you liked it." He felt her body shiver in response, and he smiled as he released her. Gianna didn't look back, and not a word left her mouth while she waited for the elevator.

The doors opened and they stepped inside, standing silently after Mayan pressed the button for his floor. Without thought, he threw his arm around her shoulders and began twirling a lock of her hair absently while he thought about what his wife needed most. *Well, I know she needs me to distract her from all the pain and sadness she's hiding. She wouldn't have pulled that shit outside if she wasn't trying to run from it.* He knew it would all eventually come crashing down around her, but he would never deny her anything she needed.

It didn't even register when he changed the direction, he was twirling her hair in. *You have to handle the business for her. No one can question her position. Our position.* He began to imagine all the horrific atrocities his gloriously unhinged wife would unleash to secure her title, and his cock thickened in response.

Looking down at her, he saw not the mask of sorrow and uncertainty that had been fastened onto her with her father's passing. Instead, he saw the wild-eyed smile of a woman who was brazenly unafraid of the monster inside her, lurking just beneath the surface.

He saw a woman who could come undone like a snake uncoiling itself from a basket and then collect herself in an instant to walk with the pride and class of the first lady. She was his everything, she was his wife.

I'll fill her in on everything the boys and I have been doing tomorrow. Tonight, she's mine. With the wheels in his mind turning furiously, he hadn't noticed the elevator stopping, or G talking. He gave her a puzzled look, and she repeated herself," Mayan, this is your floor, right?"

"Yeah. Sorry. This way," he said, taking her hand as he walked before her.

As his hand grasped the cool metal of the doorknob he stopped and looked over his shoulder at her. "I'm warning you now. I have very little control over Nickels, okay?"

She giggled and pushed into him. "I know Nickels, dummy."

Fervently believing she could never understand Nickels as a man until she experienced him, Mayan shook his head. "You don't get it, G. He's gotten even weirder. I mean, I never know what's going to come out of that fucker's mouth."

She gave him a reassuring smile, and he pushed the door open.

Mayan opened his mouth to announce their arrival, but Gianna cut him off.

She yelled out, "Hey guys! Mayan sucked on my shoe!"

His face went straight and unamused. *The audacity of this bitch.*

Mayan heard Dante make an exaggerated puking noise from the kitchen while Nickels poked his head out of his room and exclaimed, "You yelled at me for eating shit off the floor, but you can suck on shoes?!"

He shook his head emphatically. "Double standard bullshit!"

Laughing, Gianna pushed past Mayan and plopped down on the couch.

He glared at Gianna and threw his fists in the air with one finger up on each hand.

"It was one heel. One time!"

He let out a long audible exhale and smothered his hair back as he walked to join G on the couch. "And I regret nothing." He said cooly.

He sat lazily on the couch and spread out his legs while laying his arms on the back of the couch. He turned his head just in time to see Dante walk out of the kitchen. He was whipping his hands on his 'Don't make me poison you' apron and shaking his head with a look of disappointment on his face.

Dropping his apron, he placed his hands on his hips and tisked. "Ya know, you've only been married for like a week, and I'm already worried that you're a bad influence on our boy."

Gianna's jaw dropped, and she scoffed, placing her hand on her chest, but Dante continued anyway. "I certainly don't recall him sucking on any shoes before."

"He's put way worse in his mouth." Said Nickels as he walked into the living room with Poe perched on his shoulder.

Mayan jerked his chin up in Nickels's direction. "Hey! Fuck you, Nickels," he said, sneering at him openly as he pulled G closer to his side. "You're the most depraved mother fucker out of all of us." Nickels began stroking Poe's chest and staring off wistfully as Mayan continued. "Some of the shit you've done would make the devil himself blush."

Continuing to stroke Poe's chest, Nickels sighed longingly and turned towards his room. As he walked, Mayan could hear him mumbling, "Yeah, Poe, your old Pop Pop is a freak. I remember one time on the train."
And then he closed his bedroom door, leaving behind a room full of confusingly curious people.

The three of them stared at the bedroom door for about fifteen seconds before Dante clapped his hands together, breaking the awkward silence and stinging Mayan's ears.

"Well, now that Nickels has made this super weird, do you still want to stay for the dinner I made?"

Gianna's eyes snapped to Mayan, and he felt them drill through him. "I thought you said that YOU were making dinner."

Dante immediately burst out in laughter and Mayan felt his face heat with embarrassment. "Shut the fuck up, Dante. I can cook."

Dante nodded, his eyebrow raised, and his lips pursed. "Sure, " he said. "Be that as it may." He looked directly at Gianna. "G, I'm sure you don't want food poisoning."

Gianna shook her head and jabbed her elbow into Mayan's ribs. "Liar," she said through gritted teeth.

Dante took his apron off and threw it over his shoulder. He smiled wide at her. "I made baked chicken with potatoes and broccoli for the side."

They all looked over as Nickels yelled from his room. "I won't eat it! And you can't make me fox fucker!"

Dante's eyebrows bunched and his forehead wrinkled, while his shoulders scrunched up. He mouthed, "What the fuck? Fox fucker?" Then he shook his head and yelled back, "You'll eat what I make and like shit head!"

Listening to the insane fighting, Mayan put his hand over his face and cringed. Dante yelled out again as Nickels laughed, "And if you feed it to Poe one more fucking time, I swear to God, I'll cook his feathery ass next!" He threw his apron down to the ground. "Don't you push me mother fucker!"

Dante stormed away while Mayan shook his head in his hand. "Fuckin' clowns," he whispered.

Tucking herself under his arm, Gianna wrapped her arms around his torso and pushed her face into his shoulder. He looked down at her and pushed her hair from her face.

"You, okay?" he asked.

"Thank you," she whispered.

Putting his lips to the top of her head, he kissed her head and squeezed her tight.

"For what, princess?"

Gianna pulled back, and her big brown eyes sparkled as she looked up at him. "For bringing me home." She choked out. "I didn't realize how much I missed you guys. I never put it together before today.

"You all were the family I was missing." Gianna pushed her face into Mayan's shoulder again, hiding away as she said, "You are my home, Mayan."

His heart squeezed tight with her words. He couldn't remember wanting anything in this world as bad as he wanted Gianna La Rose. And now she was all his. Forever. The special moment ended abruptly when sharp pain radiated through his body from his shoulder. Gianna had bit down into the meat of his bicep. He quickly pulled away, grabbing at the pulsing bite.

"Oww, G, What the fuck?!" he yelled. Gianna spread her hand on his chest and ran it down to the top of his pants. "If you ever tell anyone I said that I'll bite it off," she said while lowering her eyes to his crotch.

A low growl rumbled from his chest as fire spread through his veins. He kept his voice low, and he bit out, "You're so fucking sexy, you psycho bitch." Then he lunged for her and gripped her hard by the waist as he stood. Her body tensed against him, and she trashed and scratched at him as he threw her over his shoulder. "That's right, princess. Keep fighting me," he cooed, as he carried her to their bedroom.

Kicking the door closed with his foot, Mayan effortlessly threw Gianna down to the bed. He ignored her grumbling while he turned on the small black lamp that sat on his nightstand.

When he turned to the bed again, the sight of her made his breath catch in his chest. There she was lying on his bed, propped up on her elbows, with her legs slightly parted.
She looked at him with lust-filled eyes beneath thick black lashes and smiled.

He was awe-struck. Mayan stood there drinking in the way the soft light illuminated the supple curves of her body.
He had never seen anything like it. He licked his lips at the delicious sight before him. The thick, black, knee-length dress had hiked up to the top of her luscious thighs, revealing the lace of her stockings squeezing tight around them. Suddenly, the nondescript was so much more provocative than it had seemed earlier.

He watched her powerful legs shift as she pushed her shoes off before bringing her dainty feet to the bed. *Fuck, there isn't an inch of her that doesn't make my dick hard. I've never been a foot guy, but I would lick and suck every fucking part of her.*

Gianna's knees slowly began to fall further apart, and her stare intensified with fiery passion. She was tempting him, teasing him until he took what he wanted. His blood heated to a boil and began racing through his veins straight to his rock-hard erection that pushed painfully against his pants. Mayan cupped his aching bulge and squeezed as he admired her sinfully beautiful body.

His voice was dark and velvet-soft when he admitted, "I can't even count how many times I thought about you lying in my bed, G." He began to rub himself through his pants, stroking with one hand and fondling his balls with the other. Goosebumps rose on his skin as her eyes fixated on his hands.

"I've laid in that bed, and stroked my cock while I imagined you…" As he spoke, Gianna's hand ran over her breast and circled it before she gripped it tight and began to knead it, making him lose his thoughts and words. The fantasy he had been trying to describe was thrown from his mind.

No fantasy he had imagined before could compare to this reality. Watching her, he wondered what her nipple would taste like if he lapped at it with his tongue when it popped out from between her slender fingers. The thought had him biting his lip as he quickly undid the buttons on his shirt and shrugged it off.

"You, Mrs. Gianna La Rosa Russo, are undeniably fucking dangerous," he said in a husky voice while removing his undershirt and unzipping his pants.

"Am I?" she asked coyly. Like a cat toying with a mouse, her hand began to work its way down her abdomen and between her thighs, forcing his eyes to follow. The overwhelming need to possess her overrode all rational thought. He would have all of her, and he would have her now.

Dropping to his knees, Mayan ran his hands over her legs, the rough callouses and scars catching on the thin fabric. A wolf-like smile spread across his face with her body's immediate reaction to his touch. His eyes met hers as he stared up at her.

"Take off the dress," he said hoarsely. Gianna panted heavily as she sat up and found the bottom of her dress to pull it up and over her head. Mayan's mouth watered as he watched her bare breasts drop out of the conservative dress.

Gianna fell back to her elbows again, and he could feel her eyes on him as he slid her black cheeky panties from her body. The temptation to taste her was too great. He pushed his face onto her inner thigh and took in a deep breath as he licked her salty skin and finished with a gentle kiss. He kept his lips to her wet skin.

"Tell me, G. Tell me what you want from me," he demanded.

A moan escaped her as her breath quickened, but she said nothing.

Disobedient brat. I swear to God, I'm really starting to believe she can't. She can't listen and obey for more than a minute, or she'll die. Opening his mouth, he began to drag the sharp edge of his teeth over the sensitive flesh of her inner thigh and put his hand on the opposite thigh.

Her legs started to close with the scrapping sensation, but Mayan tightened his grip on the soft meat of her thigh, causing her to release a small whimper with the pain.

Her hips jerked up, and she tried harder to close her legs with his head still between them. "Mayan," she panted. The predator inside him was tempted to claw its way out. But he wouldn't lose control. Not until she obeyed.

An intense rush of need rising from his center and shooting through him had Mayan pinning her knees to the bed. He panted hard, his chest rising and falling hard as he panted while staring at her pretty pussy. Adrenaline flowed, making his veins bulge and his muscles flex when he looked from her wet center to her passionate gaze.

He could barely muster more than a grunt or growl, but somehow, he managed to say it again. "Tell me what you want from me."

Gianna's abdomen flexed, and he allowed her knees to lift from the bed as she reached forward to push her fingers into his hair. Fisting his hair, she pulled, and their mouths clashed together. His tongue greedily invaded hers, reaching as far back as he could, swiping in and out, twirling his tongue around hers. She began diving deeper into his, and he rewarded her by sucking on it and catching it lightly between his teeth. Gianna pulled away and pressed her forehead to his.

He watched her face as she closed her eyes and roughly said, "I want it all Mayan. Every bit of you. Even the parts you haven't found yet. They're all mine now. Every version of you."

She grabbed his chin and pinched it as she pulled down, forcing his mouth open. Her voice deepened to a sultry purr that had precum dripping from his engorged head. "And I want this dirty fucking mouth to get to work." Tugging on his jaw, she focused on his open mouth, her hair falling to one side as she tilted her head. "I want your tongue on me, and in me. I need you to devour me."

The last wall holding the beast at bay exploded, and an animalistic growl rumbled from his chest. Pushing her back to her elbows, he forced her knees down to the bed. Saliva dripped down her leg as he bit down on the underside of her leg, just above the knee. Gianna's hoarse scream was music to his ears.

Unclenching his jaw, he moved his hand from her knee to trail his fingers along the lace of the Nylons. Lazily trailing his fingers closer to the apex of her thighs, he studied her face as she watched his hand dance its way along her leg.

Mayan groaned when he felt the heat of her center on the tips of his fingers. He lowered his head, putting his mouth right above his hand, and lightly blew, following his finger down her slick slit.

He didn't expect it when his mouth and nose were suddenly covered by her wet lips as she bucked her hips forward. Clearly, Gianna was done playing and wasn't going to ask twice. And with her sprawled out on his bed like a Sunday dinner, who was Mayan to deny her.

One deep inhale, and the primal side of Mayan scented her arousal, melting his mind. Even his inner monologue was nothing more than the grunts and groans of a feral need. With savage delight, he placed his hands on either side and buried his face in her heat.

Gianna's body jerked, twisted, and arched as he ate like a man gone crazy from starvation. Her wines, gasps, and moans mercilessly pushed him further into the outstretched arms of insanity. He sucked and nipped her clit aggressively. He plunged his tongue deep inside her before slurping up every bit of cum he extracted from her writhing body while rubbing his nose into her swollen bud.

As his need for her pleasure was satiated, the need to release himself grew exponentially. He raised his head and got to his feet while fumbling with his pants, and Gianna pushed herself further back on the bed to lay her head on a pillow. Having gotten his pants past his knees, Mayan crawled onto the bed while clumsily kicking his pants off.

Positioning himself between her legs, the head of his cock slid against her stomach, leaving a trail of precum and sending a tickle of pleasure down his spine. When he pulled back to place himself at her entrance, the delectable sensation ran through him again.

Stroking her cheek with the back of his knuckles, he softly kissed her lips.

Gianna's face was flush, and her voice softly trembled. "I love you, Mayan." The look of vulnerability on her face made his heart skip a beat.

He looked deep into her eyes and declared, "I love you, G. Don't you ever doubt that." He rubbed his cheek against hers and pushed his hand between their bodies. He laid his hand on her stomach and splayed his fingers out. His stomach clenched with fear, but he continued anyway. "I love you so much that I would give you, my life. My entire world." Rubbing her tummy, he said, "I want you to have my baby, G."

Gianna cupped his face with both hands and looked at him in a way he had never experienced. It felt like she was seeing their future together through his eyes and wanted what she saw just as badly as he did. Her legs wrapped around him, and she pulled his lips to hers. As her mouth opened to him, her feet pulled his hips into her.

He moaned into her mouth as his head pushed past her entrance and was enveloped by her wet heat. "Fuck, G. You're so tight."

Mayan slowly began pumping in and out of her rhythmically. He was kissing her neck, and her hands were roaming his body.

He pumped his hips faster and praised her when

he felt her muscles pulse around him. "Jesus. You feel amazing. The way you squeeze around me and pull me back in."

He placed his hands on either side of her and lifted himself so he could see her body beneath him. She looked like his angel of death with her hair spread out under her and her eyes flashing almost black in the low lighting. As he brought his hips back further, he felt each barbell vibrate slightly as they popped out of her.

He pushed back in, and pleasure throbbed through him as the head of his cock rubbed hard against her swollen G spot. His muscles shook with a tremor of pleasure as she pulsed around him, squeezing him hard enough that he had to thrust his hips harder to stay inside her.

Pulling back slightly, he thrust hard into her, rubbing against her G spot again as he brought his chest to hers, wrapping his arms around her tight as she moaned and arched against him. He hissed with pain as Gianna's nails dug deep into his shoulders.

Her body seized with her back arched, and she came hard around him, throwing him over the edge and into a sea of ecstasy.

His hips pushed forward and cum shot out of him with force, filling her. As he came inside her, a rush of hot liquid splashed against his balls and thighs, making him moan against her throat as her body squeezed every last drop from him.

With absolutely no more energy to give, Mayan rolled to his back and lazily threw his arm above his head. Through the haze of pleasure, he heard Gianna get up and go to his bathroom. He lay there with his eyes closed long enough to float in and out of sleep. If this is what life was going to be, then he would kill anyone who tried to take it from him.

Before he could fully fall asleep, a familiar chirp sounded from the floor, and his eyes opened. He sat up and saw G in one of his white T-shirts. She was bending over to scoop his phone from his pants pocket. She stood, waving the phone at him.

"You have a text message," she said in a snotty tone while putting a hand on her hip.

He smiled and fell back to the pillow. "You're cute, G. Open it." He lifted his head for a second to add, "It's my cousin."

As he laid his head back down, Dante's voice bellowed through the apartment. "Dinners ready, guys."

Mayan groaned and sat up, throwing his legs over the side of the bed. "If we don't go while it's hot, Mama Dante will throw a fit."

Gianna was cackling before he even finished, snorting repeatedly and trying to cover her mouth. Mayan's brow furrowed in confusion. "What the fuck is so funny?" He asked.
She forced her face to turn serious and said, "Nothing. It's time to eat." Then tossed the phone to the bed and walked to the bedroom door. Throwing it open, she yelled, "Hey guys! Did you know Mayan's cousin calls him My-My!?"

Flopping back to the bed Mayan clapped his hands over his face.

He didn't even get a chance to defend himself before all three clowns were catcalling him from the kitchen. "Heeeeeyyyyy Mhhhyyyyyyy Mhhhyyyyyy!"

He let out a growl of agitation, and grumbled through his hands, "Fucking great!"

Translations

Italian-English translations and meanings for the slang terms used:

Bellezza – Beauty

Cugina- Cousin *(feminine)*

Jadrool- is an Italian American slang term that means a loser or a bum

La Cosa Nostra- the American government's name for the Italian Mafia, also known as the Sicilian Mafia or Cosa Nostra. The term Cosa Nostra is Italian for "our thing" or "this thing of ours".

Mook- A foolish, insignificant, or contemptible person.

Principe- Prince

Principe Demone- Demon Prince

Principessa di Ghiaccio- Princess of ice (Ice Princess)

Principessa- Princess

Putana- noun. [feminine]
/pu't:ana/ vulgar. prostitute, whore.

The Outfit- The Outfit, also known as the Chicago Mafia or the Chicago Mob, is an Italian-American organized crime syndicate that originated in Chicago, Illinois in the 1910s.

Zia- Aunt

Zio- Uncle

Accompanying Music

These songs have been chosen to represent different sections of the book and characters in Cross Your Heart and Hope to Die. Me and members of my street team picked them, and we hope you enjoy them. If you would like to join the street team, please find my authors page on FB or email me at cynthiapoulosauthor@gmail.com

Apocalyptica – I don't care (for Gianna and Geo)

Chinchilla – Little girl gone (representing Gianna)

In this moment – I can be your whore

Savannah Dexter and Brabo Gator – 2 bodies

Teddy Swims – Funeral (After Mayan finally admits to himself he loves her <at the one star>)

The Cure – Lovesong (representing Mayans lonely drive)

The Menzingers – I don't want to be an asshole anymore (Mayan)

Books In This Series

"Love and Lust in the Windy City"

The Shattered Reflection

DEBUTED 5/7/2024 ~ Romance suspense. Lyla finds herself, true love, and the truth behind her emotionally abusive husband's disappearance.

Cross Your Heart and Hope to Die

DEBUTED 11/25/2024 ~ Roman's little brother, Myan, and his first love, turned enemy. A dark mafia romance.

Bake Me I'm Yours

COMING SOON ~ Tyler's world gets rocked by a baker who is a sweet snack himself. Tyler finds out there is more to Dan beneath the frosting. A sweet MM rom-com.

Devils Diamond

COMING SOON ~ Prepare yourselves. It's finally Nickels's turn to play, and he plays for keeps.